The Cats That Played the Market

Karen Anne Golden

Copyright

This book or eBook is a work of fiction. Names, characters, places and incidents are products of the author's imagination or are used fictitiously. Any resemblance to actual events, locales, persons or cats, living or dead, is entirely coincidental.

Edited by Vicki Braun.

Cover design by Christy Carlyle of Gilded Heart Design.

ISBN-13: 978-1503033276

ISBN-10: 1503033279

Dedication

To

Jeff

Acknowledgements

Thanks to Vicki Braun, my editor, who meticulously edited this book. Vicki also edited the first three books of *The Cats That . . .* Cozy Mystery series. Also, special thanks to Christy Carlyle, my book cover designer.

Thank you to my niece, Melissa McGee. Melissa and I brainstormed about plot points, sitting across from each other at my marble-top table in my Victorian living room. Melissa has an incredible eye for catching my habit of omitting words.

I want to express my appreciation to Pauline Nicolaï and Ramona Kekstadt for reading my book and offering suggestions on how to make it a better story.

Thank you, dear readers! Many of you have sent me encouraging emails and have written thoughtful reviews.

Table of Contents

Prologue

Katherine ran to her car, opened the door, and jumped in. Nervously fumbling with the clasp on her crossover bag, she extracted her cell and called Jake. "I've got an emergency," she said breathlessly. "Chief London wants me out of town."

"Why?" Jake asked in disbelief.

Katherine turned the ignition, floored the accelerator, and peeled out on Main Street. "I'm heading to the pink mansion now. I don't have time to explain."

"Katz, I'm not far. I'll meet you there and help corral the cats. We'll decide later where to go."

"Colleen's with Daryl, but her mum's home. Park in back and use your key to the basement. I'll see you in a few."

Driving in front of the house, she was shocked to see a red pickup blocking her parking spot. *Surely that's not the stolen vehicle,* she thought.

Quickly getting out of the car, she rushed up the steps to the front porch landing. She was startled when Colleen's mum opened the door.

"Hello, Katz. I was just headin' to the kitchen to make a bit of tea," she slurred.

Katherine took one whiff of Mum's breath and knew she'd been drinking. "Is everything okay?" she asked worriedly.

"Why do you ask, dear? You look like you've been touched by a banshee!"

"Whose truck is that?"

"I've been talkin' a bit of treason with your friend from the library. They're waitin' for you in the living room. I'll fix some tea."

2

Katherine took Mum by the arm. "Come with me," she insisted. She directed her to the stairwell.

Mum resisted. "Whatever 'tis the matter?"

Katherine said firmly, "Shhh! Lower your voice. Go to your room and lock the door. I only have one friend from the library, and Michelle doesn't drive a red pickup with out of state plates."

"Oh, it's somebody else. I didn't catch their name. What's goin' on?"

"I beg of you. Just do as I ask," Katherine implored. "When you get to your room, call Colleen and tell her to not come back to the house until she hears from me."

"In the name of all the saints," Mum said, as she staggered upstairs.

Katherine sprinted past Mum to her back hallway bedroom. She was alarmed to see the door standing wide-open. She had specifically shut the

3

door so the cats wouldn't bother Colleen's mum while she was away.

"Dammit," she said, surveying the room. The cats were not there. She pulled the Glock out of the gun safe and joined Mum outside her door.

"You're not goin' to use that thing, are you?" Mum said frantically. "Why don't we call the police?"

"I'm *going* to call the police! Please relax," Katherine reassured and then, with rising alarm in her voice, "*Where* are the cats?"

"The last time I saw them, they were toastin' their buns on the kitchen register."

"Hurry! Get in your room."

Mum finally went in and locked the door.

Katherine yanked her cell out of her bag and called Chief London. "I think the stolen vehicle is parked in front of my house," she said anxiously. "It's a red pickup."

"Katz, stay in your vehicle. Do NOT go inside," the chief ordered. "I'll be there in a few minutes."

"That's a problem because I'm *already* inside." She disconnected the call and tapped Jake's number. It rang and rang, then went into voice mail. "Don't come. Chief's on his way." She put the cell in her back pocket.

Gripping the Glock with both hands, she cautiously walked downstairs. Suspecting the person in the living room was armed, Katherine swiftly searched downstairs, leaving the living room for last. She had to get to the cats in the kitchen, and shut that door so they wouldn't run into the living room. Entering the kitchen, she was shocked to find the cats weren't on the register or on the window valance. *Oh, my God. They're in the living room with a murderer.*

Chapter One

Winter came early to Erie, Indiana. *The Hoosier's Almanac* had predicted mild temperatures with little precipitation. So far, however, several major storms had rolled through, dumping record snowfall. An unprecedented blizzard, unusual for this time of year, was causing havoc in the heartland. It could easily bury Erie under a foot or more of fresh powder.

Snow removal was nearly impossible because hurricane-strength winds promptly recovered surfaces. The governor declared a snow emergency for west central Indiana. People were told to stay at home. In many counties, roads were closed to the public, and were used by police, medical, and emergency vehicles only.

In Erie, there were already ten inches on the ground. The sidewalks, parking lots, streets and highways had become skating rinks.

Jake found that out the hard way. An hour before the snow emergency was declared, he left the university, where he taught, to drive home. A few miles from Erie, his blue Jeep Wrangler hit a patch of black ice and slid off the road. The Jeep bottomed out in a snow drift and broke a shock mount.

Jake called his girlfriend, Katherine — heir to the Colfax fortune — and asked if he could stay at the pink mansion for a few days. She gladly said yes, so he had a tow truck haul his Jeep to the Erie garage to be serviced.

Jake stayed overnight and slept in the guest room, down from Katherine's bedroom. He didn't sleep alone. His two feline bed buddies — Lilac and Abby — snuggled against him all night. Katherine and her three seal-point Siamese — Iris, Abra and Scout — slept together.

Jake got up early and quietly headed downstairs to the kitchen to fix Katherine breakfast. She was still asleep, so he loaded up a tray and carried it upstairs.

Abby and Lilac darted in and out of his legs as he climbed the steps. "Hey, you guys," he whispered. "Don't trip the man who has your breakfast." "Me-yowl!" Lilac protested loudly. "Quiet," he said. "Chirp," Abby cried softly. With his free hand, Jake knocked gently on Katherine's door.

Katherine was nestled under the feather comforter with Scout and Abra spooned against her. On the other side was Iris — a Siamese from a swanky pet store in Manhattan. Just one month earlier, Iris had been catnapped, but now was safe at home with her forever family. When the cats heard the tap on the door, they shot out from under the covers and launched off the bed. They knew Jake was standing outside, and from the smell that wafted underneath the door, he was bringing them food, as well.

"Wake up, sleepy heads," Jake called through the door.

"Me-yowl" and "chirp" was greeted by "waugh," "raw," and "yowl" from the other side.

Katherine sat up and said drowsily, "Come in, but be advised I look a fright in the morning."

Jake slowly opened the door. Lilac and Abby flew into the room, joining the other cats on the floor. "Happy birthday," he said, moving over and kissing Katherine on top of her head.

"You made me breakfast," she said dreamily. "And pancakes. How sweet!"

"Aunt Margie's famous recipe." He set the tray on Katherine's lap. "But first let me feed the kids." On the tray were also five fine china dishes filled with salmon paté. The cats had become very vocal and *loud*. "Here," he said, putting the dishes on the floor. "*Bon appétit!*"

"Really, I could have come downstairs," Katherine said, "but I couldn't get up. I was literally crushed to the bed by cats. Did I mention they were warm and toasty?" She laughed heartily.

"Let me pour us some coffee," Jake said, smiling, as he climbed onto the tall renaissance-revival bed.

Katherine asked, "Did you have a good night sleep? Disturbed in the night by paranormal spirits? You know that room is the haunted one."

"I was too exhausted to see a ghost," he joked. "But in the middle of the night, I woke up to the sound of something tapping on the window glass. It was this woman in white. She called me 'Heathcliff' —"

"Her name was Catherine spelled with a *C*!"

"I see you've read *Wuthering Heights*. It's kind of spooky when the wind whips around the house and the window glass rattles. That ancient wallpaper didn't help much either. Did you know that if you look at the wall long enough you can see a skull repeated in the pattern?"

"No way," Katherine countered. "That's a famous William Morris design. I never noticed it."

"Well, check it out." Jake handed her a steamy cup. "I found your stash of pumpkin spice coffee from the Covered Bridge Festival. I made a full pot so when you get dressed, we can go downstairs, drink coffee, and curl up on the loveseat.

The parlor window is featuring snow, snow and more snow," he teased.

"Ma-waugh," Scout agreed between bites.

"What does the weatherman say?"

"Nothing really dramatic," he began slowly, emphasizing each word. "We could be snowed in by mid-day. It's really coming down now. With the wind, we could have a blizzard." He then flashed his Cokenberger smile and said with a twinkle in his eye, "The University is closed today and maybe even tomorrow, which means you'll have to put up with me until the big thaw."

Katherine smiled. "I hope it doesn't thaw anytime soon."

They were interrupted by a strange sound from one of the cats: "Yum. Yum."

"Which one is doing that?" Jake asked, leaning over the bed to look down.

Katherine laughed. "The *yum yum* sound is coming from Abby. That's how she eats," she said, taking another bite of pancake oozing with thick maple syrup. "I think it's priceless."

"We'll have to cancel our trip to the city to celebrate your birthday. I already set out some steaks to thaw. I'm the official chef tonight."

"Best looking chef I've ever seen," Katherine replied playfully.

Iris, always the first cat to finish eating, jumped up on the bed. She instantly saw her opportunity and snatched a pancake off Katherine's plate. Straddling it like a multi-legged creature, she leapt off the bed. The pancake fell out of her mouth and sailed sideways like a Frisbee. Scout and Abra were right on it and collectively sprang in the air to catch it. A cat fight between two sisters erupted into multiple hisses and growls, until Abra won the altercation. She yanked the pancake out of Scout's mouth and ran down the hall with her prize.

Jake and Katherine burst out laughing. "My cats," Katherine said. "They'd do anything."

*   *   *

In the late afternoon, Jake trudged to the carriage house and found a snow shovel. He cleared a path back to the pink mansion. He removed snow on the front porch and sidewalk as well, but fresh powder quickly recovered it. Katherine gazed out the window at the winter spectacle while Scout and Abra sat on the windowsill, standing on their hind legs trying to capture snowflakes through the glass. It brought back a memory of the previous winter when she watched for Mark Dunn, the estate attorney, to arrive. *So much has happened since then*, she reflected. She'd moved from a busy metropolis to the slow pace of a town where everyone knew each other, and all local businesses

15

except the bars shut down by nine o'clock. And she'd fallen in love with Jake Cokenberger.

Mark was in the process of closing his Erie law office to move to Indianapolis and join a large firm. He was still representing her great aunt Orvenia's estate, and would continue until the final distribution in less than two months. He telephoned or texted, but it was business-related, seldom personal. He might ask about the cats once in a while, particularly Abby. The well-being of Abby was paramount to Katherine's inheriting the Colfax fortune. No Abby, no inheritance.

A few weeks earlier, Mark had been at Katherine's side, during the Patricia Marston murder trial. Because of a change of venue, the case wasn't tried in Erie, but in neighboring Shaleville, in Brook County. Patricia was charged with the murder of Katherine's ex-boyfriend, Gary, as well as her own mother, the former housekeeper, Vivian. The murders had taken place in late February, and didn't come to trial until ten months later.

Katherine had to testify about discovering the two bodies. It was extremely stressful to recount those awful events, and to be in the same room with a woman who had caused so much sorrow. When the prosecuting attorney asked Katherine about the jimson seeds, which Patricia had placed in food, intending to poison her, Patricia stood up and started yelling obscenities. The judge ordered her attorney to silence his client, but Patricia threatened Katherine, "Wait and see what I do to you!" Members of the jury were shocked by the outburst. The judge recessed for the day and asked to speak to counsel in his chambers. He advised Patricia's lawyer that he should rein in his client's verbal displays to prevent further criminal charges.

On the next day, Cokey Cokenberger, the estate's handyman, was called to the stand to answer questions about his brief affair with Patricia —

particularly how she used him to get in and out of

the mansion. Patricia went ballistic and called Cokey

a liar. Cokey's wife Margie glared at Patricia. The

judge had grown furious. "Ms. Marston, if I hear one

more word out of you, I'll have you removed from

this courtroom."

"I don't care," Patricia said. "I'm a dead

woman walking." The outburst sealed her fate. The

jury deliberated for less than two hours. The only

evidence they wished to revisit was the coroner's

toxicology report. When they returned to the

courtroom, they found Patricia guilty on all counts.

Patricia's sentencing was scheduled for

today, but Katherine opted not to go and asked Mark

to attend in her place. He said he'd call as soon as he

learned something.

When the house telephone rang, Katherine

flinched. She moved to the atrium marble-top curio

cabinet to answer it. "Hello," she answered anxiously, hoping it was Mark.

"Hey, Katz. It's Mark. Happy birthday," he said. "How does it feel to be twenty-seven?"

"Hi, Mark. It feels like being twenty-six," she laughed, then asked seriously, "I take it the sentencing was postponed because of the weather."

"Brook County isn't part of the snow emergency so the courthouse is open. I'm sorry I couldn't be there in person, but I just got a call from the Prosecutor . . . "

Katherine interrupted, "What's the sentence?"

"The judge threw the book at her. She got maximum for Gary's and her mother's murders. She'll spend the rest of her miserable life in prison, with little or no chance of parole."

Katherine sighed. "I don't know what to say.

That I'm happy? That I'm glad? What she took from

this world can never be replaced."

"I'm truly sorry," Mark consoled. "Chief

London said she'll be transferred from the Brook

County Jail to the women's correctional facility in

Indy. It's a done deal, Katz. Do you want me to call

Gary's sister, Monica, and tell her the verdict?"

"No, Mark, I will. Thanks for calling —"

"Before you hang up," Mark interrupted. "I

have a birthday surprise for you. Will you be home

in the next half-hour? I want to bring it over to you."

"You really shouldn't have," Katherine said,

"but I'm flattered you remembered my birthday.

How did you know, anyway? My Facebook page,

bank documents . . . "

"Oh, a little birdie told me," Mark laughed

on the other end.

"One that flies in Manhattan," Katherine said in jest, realizing her best friend, Colleen, must have told him the previous month when Mark drove her to the airport.

"Guilty," Mark said. "Be there in a minute," he said hanging up.

Katherine tried to put the phone down, but Scout came out of nowhere and kicked the receiver out of her hand.

"Scout, what's the matter with you? Gimme the phone," she said, wrestling the instrument from the Siamese's strong paws.

Jake knocked and opened the front door. He came in and stamped his boots on the hall mat. Iris ran to greet him, then began patting the snow that fell from his boots. With her deep-blue eyes, she looked up at Katherine and seemed to say, "What's this, Mom? It's cold on my paws."

"Katz, are you okay?" Jake asked, concerned. "You're three shades of gray."

"I just got off the phone with Mark Dunn. Patricia Marston got the maximum sentence on each of the murder counts. Life in prison without parole." She moved away, her jaw tightening.

Jake walked over to Katherine and pulled her into an embrace. "Finally, you have closure."

Katherine gave a forced smile and hugged him back.

"Oops, I forgot to take off my boots," he apologized.

Iris was now rolling on the snow tracks. She abruptly stopped, then rolled on her back and kicked her paws in the air.

Katherine broke into a laugh. "I think she likes it."

Jake walked back to the front vestibule and took off his boots, placing them on a large boot mat next to the door. He then announced, "The kids and I are baking you a cake."

"Get outta here," Katherine said with a loving look on her face.

"Yep, headin' to the kitchen now, but just want to warn you in advance, it will be a surprise, this masterpiece cake, so you'll have to find something to do and stay out of our way," he said, walking in his stocking feet to the kitchen, with Iris on his heels.

"That shouldn't be hard to do," Katherine called after him. "Mark Dunn said he had a surprise for me and was stopping by."

Jake stopped. "A surprise? Don't tell me he's baking you a cake, too," he said mischievously.

"That's for me to know and you to find out."

"How's he going to get here in that Honda he drives when the snow plows can't even keep up?"

Katherine shrugged. "It's a mystery."

*   *   *

The front doorbell rang with a festive holiday ringtone. "Dashing Through the Snow" had replaced the Addams Family "You Rang." Katherine got up from an Eastlake chair to open it. Mark stood outside, shivering in his faux fur-lined parka. Katherine looked past him at an older model Ford Explorer.

"Come in," she said, opening the door wider. "Did you get a different vehicle?"

Mark walked in. "It's my dad's. My parents are vacationing in Florida. Since I'm minding their house, he let me borrow the Explorer. It has four-wheel drive."

Mark sat down on the vestibule's Eastlake

bench and removed his boots, placing his pair next

to Jake's on the boot mat. He gave Katherine an

inquisitive look.

Katherine read his mind, "Jake's snowed in,

so he's staying with me for a few days."

"Where is he?" Mark said with a smile.

"He'll want to be in on the surprise, as well."

"Jake and the cats are baking me a cake," she

announced with a wide grin. "I can go get him."

"Yes, please do." Iris ran in and collapsed

against Mark's leg. He picked her up and gave her

chin scratches. Iris yowled affectionately.

Katherine smiled. "Mark, hand me your

parka."

Mark set Iris down and slipped off his coat.

Katherine took it and said, "Make yourself

comfortable in the parlor. I'll go get Jake." She hung the parka on the Eastlake hall tree and left.

Mark sat on the loveseat in front of the wide picture window. Katherine returned, holding Jake's hand.

"Hey, Mark," Jake said, dropping Katherine's hand and extending his to Mark.

Mark shook it. Jake found a chair nearby and Katherine sat opposite him. Scout and Abra strolled in, with a hint of flour on their velvet noses. Lilac and Abby jumped up smoothly to the large window valance and perched like vultures.

Katherine observed the cats and said, "I think the cats want to be in on the surprise, as well," and then, "I don't see a pony, or any wrapped presents. The suspense is killing me."

Mark reached inside his zipped fleece pull-on and pulled out a check. "I had the bank cut a distribution check just in time for your birthday," he said, holding the check.

Jake and Katherine exchanged inquiring glances.

"Katz," Mark continued, "since it's obvious you have satisfied and will satisfy the requirements of your late great aunt Orvenia's will, I am authorized to give you this check in the amount of five million dollars."

Katherine's mouth dropped. Suddenly the reality of inheriting a huge fortune hit her like a ton of bricks. She was momentarily speechless.

"Ma-waugh," Scout cried, breaking the silence. She jumped on Katherine's lap and wrapped her slender, brown paws around her neck.

"Ahhh, thanks, Scout," Katherine said, as Scout made herself comfortable on her lap, circling two times, then lying down.

27

"Katz, what a special birthday present," Jake remarked, without something better to say. He was in shock, too.

"The estate will receive some tax advantages by making this distribution before the year ends. Actually, by giving you this money now, the bank's trust department will be doing the estate a favor."

Katherine was still reeling in the shock of reality. Mark stood up and placed the check in her hand. She gazed at it in disbelief. Finally she stuttered, "Thank you. And thanks for bringing it over in this horrid weather."

Mark said, "I need for you to sign this receipt, then you're good to go." He extracted a small document from his fleece jacket, and handed it to her along with his Pelikan fountain pen. When Katherine leaned forward to take the receipt, Scout didn't like being disturbed, so she sprang off and cried a barrage of Siamese mutterings that only the other cats seemed to understand.

Katherine signed the receipt and handed it back to Mark. He put the pen back in his pocket. "Katz, since it's your money, you can do with it whatever you want. But there's a new financial advisor in town — straight from Wall Street — and he has some interesting investment ideas. You could easily triple your money. I've already invested." Mark handed Katherine the advisor's business card, which she accepted.

She read, "G. Robert Brentwood, 531 Fifth Avenue, Twentieth Floor, New York, New York. Why is someone of this caliber in Erie?" she asked.

"Robert's mother lives here. He's moved in to care for her. She's eighty-nine and needs someone at the house. As long as Robert has Wi-Fi, he can work at home. By the way, his mom, Elizabeth, hung out with your great aunt. In fact, they were best friends back in the day."

"Really?" Katherine asked. "I'd love to meet her."

"She's in a band; they play the senior centers in this area."

"I've met her," Jake added. "When I was writing my dissertation, I interviewed her. She was too young to remember Prohibition, but she gave me a lot of local information about the swing era."

"The swing era?" Katherine asked. "When was that?"

Jake explained. "The swing era is also referred to as the big band era. That's when Elizabeth hung out with Orvenia. In the Forties."

"Cool," Katherine remarked, then asked Mark, "I have a question about the Erie properties my great aunt left me in her will. Is there any way I can have a portfolio for each one, including the estate's appraisals, property taxes and zoning rules?" She thought, *I wonder if any of these properties could house the new, no-kill animal rescue center I'm planning to finance.*

"Sure, give me a couple of days and I'll compile that for you," he said, standing up. "I've got to head home and answer a ton of emails. Katz, I'll text you Elizabeth's phone number. I'll have the Colfax properties summary to you as soon as possible."

Katherine and Jake walked Mark to the door. Iris followed them and yowled softly.

"Goodbye, Iris. Hope to see you soon." Mark pulled on his boots. Katherine handed him his parka, and then the estate attorney left with a smile on his face.

"Katz, this is your special day. Money, cake, and me. What more could you ask for?" Jake kidded.

"Maybe I should call this Brentwood guy and see what he has to say. Tripling my money sounds like a good thing. I've got lots of ideas about how I'm going to spend the inheritance. I'll call him and schedule a time to meet."

Jake looked at his watch. His brown eyes grew big. "I forgot the cake!"

In the kitchen, the smoke alarm blared its sharp, irritating screech. Iris, Lilac and Abby thundered upstairs to avoid the sound.

The smell of smoke floated through the air. Jake and Katherine bolted to kitchen. While Katherine climbed on the kitchen footstool to disable the alarm, Jake opened the oven door. A thick, black cloud rose from what remained of the masterpiece cake. "I think I need to edit what I just said. How about money and me? I'll have to bake another cake. Cats? Where are my helpers?"

Scout and Abra sprinted in with their upper lips curled. "Waugh," Scout coughed. The two hiked up their tails and trotted off to another room.

Katherine sat down on the kitchen chair and laughed until her side hurt. "I'll help you," she said. "Where's the recipe?"

Chapter Two

Cokey drove his new Dodge Ram, equipped with a snow blade, to the mansion and plowed the driveway, so that Katherine could move her Subaru out from under the covered carport. She drove Jake to the garage to pick up his Jeep so he could drive to the university, where he taught a one o'clock class. Katherine was meeting G. Robert Brentwood, the financial advisor, who had an office in Mark Dunn's building downtown. As she pulled into a parking space and got out of her car, a very tall, barrel-chested man approached her.

"Are you Katherine Kendall? I'm G. Robert Brentwood. Just call me Robbie. I'm so glad to meet you. Did you have any trouble getting here? What do you think of this weather? Mark said you were from New York. Have you been there lately?"

Katherine just stared at the man with her mouth open because he asked a million questions and didn't give her time to answer any of them.

"I'm on the second floor," Robbie continued in a thundering voice. "Mark Dunn is also on my floor. You know him, of course. He's your late aunt Orvenia's lawyer. Here, I'll show you the way."

He held the lobby door open and continued, "I'm so sorry. I haven't let you get a word in edge-wise. My mother says it's a terrible habit of mine. Please, let's take the stairs. I need the exercise."

Katherine agreed. He carried an unhealthy amount of weight. On the second floor, Robbie escorted Katherine to a small office with sparse furnishings. There was a desk and office chair, computer, and combination printer and fax machine. Against the windowed wall was a credenza with mounds of paper stacked on it. Obviously, Robbie's forte wasn't filing.

"Please have a seat," Robbie said, pointing at a leather-covered side chair. He sat behind his desk and immediately began nervously twiddling with a pen. "Mark has told me that you are interested in investing. I'm privy to a new, high-performing mutual fund that is paying off in big bucks. I also do direct management of investments for high-net worth individuals like you."

Katherine took a deep breath and wondered when the man would let her talk. "I would like to hear more about it." She plucked another business card from a holder near the edge of the desk. The reverse side of the card had raised, bold letters spelling out Licensed Financial Professional.

"It's as simple as this," Robbie continued. "You give me the sum of 'x' dollars. I'll set up an account at the Erie bank of your choice. You'll give me access to the money and I'll make decisions on what to buy and what to sell. I guarantee within three months, I will have tripled your money."

"In this economy, you must do very well with what you do," Katherine remarked. She glanced at the wall, which held three mat-framed diplomas: an undergraduate degree from a university in New Jersey, an MBA degree from a prestigious school, and a certificate identifying him as a certified financial planner.

"I worked on Wall Street for a number of years and I'm aware of the best investment opportunities available on today's market. In fact, I still have an office in Manhattan."

"Interesting," Katherine noted. "As a matter of fact, when I worked in midtown, your building was very close to mine —"

Robbie interrupted, throwing his hands up in excitement. He said in a booming voice, "We could

have bumped into each other and not even known it.
As I was saying," he returned to the topic at hand,
"If you sign this account agreement and deposit a
mere five thousand dollars I will begin my magic.
I'm sure you'll be so happy with the results."

Katherine thought, *Mom used to say if it
looks too good to be true, then it probably is.* "I'd
like to explore your offer further. Do you have a
website I can access? Any literature I can study?"

"I assure you, what I do is completely
legitimate," Robbie said, undaunted, "I will invest a
major part of your money in this new mutual fund,
and you'll see the windfall within a month or two.
The more you put in, the more you make. Easy
sneezy," he said. "Everyone in Erie is investing.
Why not jump on the bandwagon today?"

Katherine thought, *What a salesman! He
won't take no for an answer.* Standing up to leave,
she gathered her bag and folded her coat over her

arm. She smiled politely. "I'll take this under advisement and get back to you. Thank you so much for meeting with me." She stepped for the door, but Robbie stood up and called her back.

"Oh, by all means. Here's my website," he said, scratching the address on the back of one of his business cards, which she already had, but accepted this one, as well. "Check it out! Check me out! And don't delay. Get back to me right away!"

Katherine hurriedly headed for the elevator bank. A line had formed outside Robbie's office door. She recognized the mayor's wife and Cokey Cokenberger.

"Hi, Cokey," she said, stopping to talk. "I want to thank you for plowing my driveway this morning." She knew it was a lame excuse to talk to him, because she had already thanked him earlier. She was curious why he'd want to meet with the new financial advisor in town.

"You're welcome, Katz," he said, then whispered. "I heard I can triple my investment in a matter of months, so I'm investing big-time."

Katherine's eyes grew wide. "Oh, Cokey, is that wise? Have you investigated this man's credentials?"

Cokey shrugged and said dismissively, "No big deal, but don't tell Margie. I want it to be a surprise."

Katherine looked skeptical. "I guess." Mark Dunn was coming out of his office and literally bumped into her.

"Fancy meeting you here," he said amicably. "I take it you took my advice and met with Mr. Brentwood."

"Yes," she said non-committedly. "I know you said you'd invested money with him, but I need to think about it."

"Don't wait too long," Mark advised. "I was just heading for lunch. Care to join me?"

"Oh, Mark, I'd love to, but can I take a rain check? I'm meeting Michelle from the library. We're having lunch at the diner."

"Okay . . . hang on a second. I've got those property documents for you." He dashed back in his office to get them. He returned, holding a three-ring binder with side tabs peeking out along the edge. "Any questions, just give me a call."

"I appreciate it," Katherine said, walking with him to the elevator.

When the doors swished open on the first floor, Mark's cell phone rang. He stopped to answer it, then said to Katherine, "Catch you later."

Katherine smiled and made her way out of the building. As she opened the front lobby door, she was forced to move aside by a very angry man who was cursing to himself. "When I get a hold of that lyin' son of a bitch, I'm gonna snap his neck in two," the man said, storming for the elevator bank. She heard Mark say, "Hey, Nick, let's calm down there, buddy."

Wow! I guess I'm leaving just in time, Katherine thought. *Wonder what that was all about? Wonder who Nick is?*

Once outside, Katherine slid on a patch of ice and instantly righted herself. She thought she was getting very good at this and wondered if there was a special category in the Olympics for such an athletic skill. The town of Erie couldn't keep up with the streets, let alone clear the sidewalks. She climbed in her Subaru and drove to the diner. She parked close to the door and walked inside. Michelle had reserved a booth in the far corner. She waved Katherine over.

"Hey, Katz, how are you? Long time, no see."

"Where does the time go?" Katherine said, sliding into the booth.

"How's your new computer class going? Any serial killers enrolled this time?" Michelle said, tongue-in-cheek, referring to her disastrous date with the Festival Murderer himself.

"I have four super students. The session is almost finished, but I'm going to take a month off before the next group."

Frank, the waiter, came over and took their orders. He repeated, "For you, Katz, one Reuben with extra sauerkraut. And for you, Michelle, one breaded pork tenderloin with mayo and dill pickles."

"Oh, Frank, could you add a spring water for me?" Katherine asked.

"Yeppers," he said, smiling. "Michelle, the same?"

"Yep. Thanks, Frank. Oh, by the way, how's your mom doing? I heard she was in the hospital," Michelle asked, concerned.

"She fell and broke her hip, but the doc patched her up. She'll be dancing the jig in no time." He grinned and walked away.

Michelle smirked, "Frank's mom is a hoot. You've got to meet her. She'll be at the annual holiday fundraiser, I'm sure. She makes these white chocolate cakes in clay flowerpots. They are to die for! Oh, by the way, Katz, you never got back to me. Are you attending, or not? I'm organizing it this year and I've reserved a table for you, but you never gave me the heads up."

"I've given it much thought, but what can I make to sell for charity?"

Frank brought the spring water over and poured each a glass. After he left, Michelle said,

"Well, Orvenia always baked her famous iced sugar cookies. They were made from butter and were absolutely delicious. Why don't you try that?"

Katherine chuckled to herself, remembering baking the 'masterpiece' birthday cake with Jake. She wondered if he'd help her make the cookies. "That's not a bad idea, Michelle," Katherine said enthusiastically. "I found her cookbook in the attic, of all places. I'll look for the sugar cookie recipe. Wouldn't it be fun if I cut them in the shape of cats?"

Michelle giggled, "Purrfect!"

All of a sudden, the loud din of gossiping Erie townspeople came to a screeching halt. The entrance door bell sounded, which indicated somebody new had entered. There was dead calm. Katherine had her back to the door and whispered across the table to Michelle, "Who just came in?" She wore a knowing grin on her face about the town's practice of sizing up a newcomer before resuming their idle talk, a.k.a. gossip.

Michelle whispered back, "Look out! It's Barbie Sanders and she's headed this way."

"Really?" Katherine asked, turning in her seat. "Barbie, how are you?" Katherine was surprised to see her former student in a navy-blue business suit with a crisp white blouse. Her hair was pulled back in a ponytail and she wore little make-up.

"I'm just fine, Teach," Barbie said. "I'd bring you an apple, but I ate it on the way. Oh, ha! Ha!"

All heads were turned in their direction, and then like magic, the gossipers started talking again.

"Want to join us?" Katherine asked.

Barbie slid in next to Katherine. "I'd love to, but I can only stay a few minutes. Katz, I saw your car parked outside so I wanted to come in and give you the news. I'm moving to the city. Daddy rented me an apartment. I just interviewed for a part-time job at a small animal clinic and I got accepted at the technical college."

"Woo-hoo! I'm so proud of you," Katherine said, genuinely happy for her privately taught student, who turned out to be a whiz at computers. "What are you going to major in?"

"Just general business courses at first, but I want to be a vet tech."

Katherine remembered how much Barbie loved cats, and how well she took care of Iris when the Siamese was stolen, then abandoned in Barbie's trailer court. "You'll be perfect."

"I also want to show you my baby pictures." Barbie rooted around in her Coach bag and pulled out a baby book.

"When did you have a baby?" Michelle asked.

Barbie ignored the question and handed the book to Katherine, who began thumbing through the photos.

"Oh," Katherine gushed. "Seal-point kittens. How old are they?"

"They're twelve-weeks-old. I named them Dewey and Crow."

"Where did you get them?" Katherine asked.

"Look out, Katz. You've already got a bunch," Michelle warned.

Barbie continued, "Daddy drove me to Chicago to a gal friend of his. Her friend breeds Siamese. Oh, you would have not believed it. The entire house was full of Siamese, and kittens everywhere. It was hard for me to pick, but when I saw the two brothers playing, I had to have them."

Frank brought their sandwiches over, set the plates down, and eyed Barbie curiously. Barbie said haughtily, "Take a picture, Frank. It lasts longer."

Frank rolled his eyes and left.

"I'll leave you two to your lunch," Barbie said as she stood up. "I'm headin' home to pick up the rest of my stuff. Take care now," she added, leaving.

Michelle gave Katherine a surprised look. "I'm impressed. Business suit and all."

"I suggested to Barbie that she attend a business attire/etiquette class, and apparently she took me up on it. Did you notice she didn't have the obnoxious, loud laugh?"

"I kind of heard it once," Michelle corrected. "But it was much more subdued than usual."

Katherine agreed. "I'm going to have company in a few days. My friend Colleen and her

49

mother are flying in. I'll have to ask them if they want to contribute to the fundraiser as well."

"Sweet! The more the merrier! Okay, I've got you marked off to make Katz's Kitty Cat cookies. Let me know what Colleen and her mom want to do."

"I will. I'll text Colleen and ask later."

"Fun!"

They both dug into their sandwiches and agreed to meet again for lunch later in the week.

* * *

After lunch, Katherine drove into the city to run some errands, then returned to Erie with a car load of groceries. As she pulled into the carport, she saw five cats sitting on the wide windowsill in the dining room. Clearly, they had been waiting for her to return home. She didn't know if they were genuinely happy to see her, or if they knew inside one of those grocery bags was dinner — a premium gourmet feast. It was a toss between the two.

When she turned the key in the side door and walked through the vestibule to the dining room, the cats met her with great anticipation and noise as they voiced their happiness at her arrival.

"Inside voices, please," Katherine said, struggling with two bags of groceries. "Let me feed you guys as soon as possible so you'll give my ears a rest."

She set the bags on the glass-top Parsons table and stepped back to bring in more, but stopped when the kitchen phone rang. She answered it on the second ring. She would have answered it earlier, but Scout pounced on the phone and she had to wrestle the cat for the receiver. "Again, Scout? Stop it!" she scolded the rambunctious Siamese. "Hello," she said into the mouthpiece.

"Stop it?" an elderly female voice said. "What did I do?"

"Oh, I'm so sorry. Who's calling please?"

"Is this Orvenia's niece?"

"Great niece, yes."

"I'm Elizabeth Brentwood. Friends call me Lizard. My son mentioned you the other day and gave me your number. I bet you didn't know it, but I used to run around town with your aunt."

"Great aunt," Katherine corrected in a friendly tone. "Mark Dunn gave me your number, but I haven't had a chance to call. I never met my great aunt. I'd love to hear about her. Would you like to come for tea?" Katherine added at the spur of the moment.

"Oh, I'd love to. I've been in your home many times and it would be swell to see it again. But you must understand, I don't drive anymore. My chauffeur is my son, Robbie. Is it okay if he comes, too? We can give him a cookie or two and he'll retreat to the corner," the woman continued in a raspy voice.

"Yes, of course. I met your son the other day. How about this Friday? Say four o'clock?"

"I'll write it on my calendar, and I'll be there. Thank you so much for inviting us." Elizabeth, also known as Lizard, hung up.

Katherine turned to find five annoyed cats starring up at her from the ceramic floor. Scout's and Abra's tails were thrashing in unison — thumpity thump thump.

"Okay, I surrender, Dorothy," Katherine said. "I'll feed you now."

"Yowl," Iris cried in her sweetest voice.

"Yes, Miss Siam, I do believe I'll give you a bit more for being my darling girl." Katherine picked up the seal-point and gave her a kiss on the back of her neck.

The telephone rang again and Katherine moved to answer it. "I'm sorry, kids. Next time, I promise I'll let it go to voice mail."

"Hello," she answered.

"Is this Katherine Kendall?" the male voice boomed on the other end.

"Yes, is this Mr. Brentwood?" She recognized the loud voice, and held out the receiver to protect her ear.

"Oh, we don't have to be so formal. Call me Robbie. Listen, I just wanted to stop by for a minute. I'm the new volunteer curator of the Erie Historical Museum, and I'm returning a few boxes of material belonging to your great aunt — items we didn't use."

"What kind of items?"

"Tons of photographs. I think your great aunt kept the Kodak people happy."

"Sure, I'm home now," Katherine said. "Any time is fine."

The combination curator/financial advisor continued, "On behalf of the Erie Historical Society, I want to thank you for your outstanding donation of the late Orvenia and William Colfax's memorabilia. I'm sure you won't be disappointed with how I plan to display them, but I need to ask you a few questions about certain items — just by way of clarification. I can be at your house in ten minutes. Okay, then," he said, without giving Katherine time to answer. "I'll see you shortly."

Before Katherine could answer, Robbie hung up.

He's the pushiest man I've ever met, she thought.

Scout had jumped to the counter and was pawing the phone. "Waugh," she cried irritably.

"Scout, speak English, please. I don't know what you're trying to tell me — other than you're starving — but that was Mr. Motormouth. I've gotta feed you cats pronto, before he shows up."

*   *   *

The new volunteer curator parked in front of the mansion. He drove a late-model four-door Lexus. Katherine met him at the door and let him in. He was holding what looked like a portfolio under his arm, and two cardboard boxes stacked on top of each other.

"Hello, Robbie," Katherine said. "You can set the boxes down anywhere."

He placed them on the floor inside the vestibule.

Katherine asked curiously, "What's in them?"

"One box is full of family photographs we weren't able to use. You should have them. But in the second box," he said, reaching down and taking off the lid, "is a valuable antique you should keep." He pulled out an ancient stock market ticker tape machine.

"That's really cool," Katherine said. "When I cleaned out the attic, I don't remember finding it."

"Oh, my mother had it. She said she got it from your great aunt in the Forties. Orvenia said she hated to look at it, because it brought back sad memories. Your great uncle was supposedly obsessed with the machine. Orvenia was going to throw it away, but my mother talked her into giving it to her."

"Interesting," Katherine said. "I love these little tidbits of family history. I guess in modern times, it would be like your husband watching sports all the time, or constantly checking his cell phone."

"Exactly! My mother donated it to the museum, but Ms. Kendall, this machine is too valuable for our current insurance policy. I did preliminary research. It's worth over ten thousand dollars."

Katherine's mouth dropped. "Amazing. Maybe we should leave it in the box until I can find a place for it. I don't want the cats to break it."

"Yes, because it's the real McCoy," Robbie said, then continued, "I absolutely love this house. When I was a little boy I used to spend hours playing in the attic while my mom and your great aunt chatted below. In fact, I'm the guilty one who carved his initials on the wall up there."

"I've never seen it," she said. "Let me take your coat. We can sit in the living room," she guided.

The heavy-set man chose the rare, expensive Rococo Belter chair — the most fragile chair in the room. Katherine cringed and hoped it wouldn't collapse. It was already too late to suggest a safer, *less-expensive* chair. Katherine hoped she didn't have to add its demise to the growing list of broken or destroyed items. Mark Dunn required a list for insurance purposes. Katherine sat down opposite Robbie on the mauve-colored loveseat.

Robbie smiled and asked, "For your great aunt and uncle's exhibit, I was wondering if a graphic artist friend of mine could come over and photograph the two portraits in here?"

"I think Orvenia and William would be honored. Have him call me to set up a time."

"Actually, she. Emily Bradworth works for a designer in the city and has volunteered to do this. She'll take photos, then enlarge them into posters. I just thought it would be fabulous to have their portraits hanging on the wall above the museum display case."

"I'm kind of confused," Katherine said. "The museum's opening is in a week, would Ms. Bradworth have time to do this?"

"Emily is a fast worker. It's just a matter of her photographing the portraits, then going back to the studio and doing her thing."

"It sounds good to me. I can't wait to see what you've done with the Colfax material. You said on the phone you needed to clarify some info about my family."

"Oh, yes," he said, pulling a small notepad out of his pocket. "Where was your great aunt born?"

"Brooklyn," Katherine answered. "Bay Ridge."

"William Colfax was born in Erie. Do you know how he met your great aunt? The more personal details, the more people will be interested in the display."

"My granny said my great aunt was a hatcheck girl at the Waldorf-Astoria. William was in town for business and met her there. That's all I know, except she was seventeen."

"Yes, there was quite an age difference. I just met a client for lunch at the Waldorf."

Katherine nodded and wondered if she could hurry him along.

Robbie repositioned himself on the Belter chair, which creaked loudly. He seemed to not notice. "I heard you had cats, but I don't see any," he said, changing the subject. He scanned the room. "I love cats."

Gazing through one of the open pocket doors, Katherine thought she saw the shadow of Scout or Abra in the vicinity of the Eastlake hall tree, where she had hung Robbie's coat. But when she looked harder, she didn't see them, or any of the other cats. "Oh, they're probably plastered on the heat register in the kitchen. In this weather, that's where they like to hang out," she explained.

"Ha, ha!" he boomed, and in a jovial mood added, "Before I leave, I've taken the liberty of preparing a portfolio about an incredible investment opportunity, available here only through me." He speedily placed several documents on the coffee table in front of Katherine. "I have direct access to this new fund, which was founded by some top money managers in New York. There is a complete prospectus here, and some standard subscription forms. I realize you're inclined to be skeptical about such investments, but I can personally guarantee you'll be very happy with the returns you'll quickly earn. My clients receive a monthly statement of their financial growth." He gave a wide-open smile and placed a felt-tip pen on the documents.

When Katherine leaned over to look at the papers, she again saw movement in the corner of her eye, but when she turned in that direction, she observed a whirlwind of Siamese cats chasing each other. Iris was in the lead, carrying a small envelope in her teeth. She dodged Scout and Abra by darting underneath the infamous wingback chair — Abby's storage place for stolen loot, which had now become Iris's cache, as well. Scout and Abra couldn't brake soon enough. They skirted the coffee table, scattered the papers, and came to a skidding halt several feet

away, then began hissing and snarling at each other.

Iris — now inside the wingback chair — emitted a

deep growl. Abra boxed Scout's ears and then raced

off with one of the ripped sheets of paper clamped in

her jaws, with Scout trailing after her. Robbie sat

back in his chair, which moaned as if it were in its

final death throes. He wore a shocked look on his

face. Clearly, he'd never witnessed a Siamese

stampede.

Katherine apologized, "I'm sorry. I don't

know what got into them. Would you be so kind as

to reprint the documents?" She got up from her

chair, "Now, if you'll excuse me, I have an

appointment in the city." Actually there wasn't an

appointment. She just wanted the verbose financial

advisor to leave.

"Yes," he said, getting up and heading to the

door.

Katherine swiftly picked up his coat, which was now lying in a heap on the floor. A trace of cream and brown cat fur was enough proof that the Siamese had pulled the coat down from the hall tree. She brushed it off as best she could and handed it to him. "I'm so sorry, again. My cats have been very busy today."

"Ha, ha! No problem," Robbie bellowed.

Opening the front door, Katherine said, "I look forward to seeing you and your mother in a few days. Maybe you can bring the documents then?"

"Yes," he said, then launched into another sales pitch. All Katherine could hear was "Yadda, Yadda." Lilac trotted around the corner and began me-yowling loudly. Her Siamese voice was so shrill that Robbie seemed to be relieved to walk out the door. After he left, Katherine picked up the lilac-point and said, "Good work. You deserve a chin scratch for that."

Iris, Scout and Abra returned to the room.

Abra dropped the now-mutilated page on

Katherine's shoe, looked up with blinking eyes, and

cried a sweet, innocent "raw."

Reaching down to pick up the torn, crumpled

document, Katherine said to the cats, "Okay, I get it.

You don't want me to invest with this man. I hadn't

planned on it anyway. Oh, and Miss Siam, I saw you

stash something in the chair. Let's go have a peek

and see what it was."

Iris protested with a loud yowl. Katherine

walked back to the living room and got down on her

hands and knees. A rusty brown paw extended from

inside the torn lining. "Abby, get out of there." The

Abyssinian hopped out and "chirped" before moving

aside to stand guard while her person searched

through her stuff.

Katherine began removing stolen items from

the chair. Abby and Iris had clearly moved up in the

world. They were collecting more expensive items. Basic household items and toiletries had been replaced with objects of value: Katherine's missing silver earring, a gold chain, and a small ivory envelope. A fang mark blessed the corner. She removed the blank card and began to read the almost illegible handwriting. "Oh, Robbie darling, why can't we announce our engagement at the museum opening? I do love you so much, Emily."

"Emily," Katherine said out loud to the cats, which had gathered around her. "Emily Bradworth, the graphics designer, perhaps? Cats of mine, how am I going to return this to Robbie? It's very personal. I can't just give it to him and explain how you punks stole it."

Scout, a no-nonsense kind of cat, snatched the card from her hand and ran to the front door. With long, slender brown paws she pushed the card through the mail slot. "Waugh," she cried.

Katherine giggled and went to retrieve the card from the other side of the door. "Okay, I'll just mail it anonymously. Who wants a treat?" she asked.

With the sound of that magic word, five felines thundered to the kitchen. The collected sound of pounding paws on the wood floor and caterwauling was almost earsplitting. Katherine followed and smiled happily as she yanked the cat treat package out of the cabinet and handed each one of her cats a delicious treat.

Heading to her office, she observed that one of the cats had walked across her keyboard and woke up the computer from sleep mode. The screen was the log-in page for an e-trading company.

"Which one of you did this?" she called to the cats in the kitchen. She sat down and researched the company. She decided it might be beneficial to set up an account. She entered a user name and password, then was distracted by a strong feeling that G. Robert — Robbie — Brentwood wasn't on the up-and-up. She didn't trust him.

She opened her desk drawer, retrieved Robbie's business card, and then extracted her cell from her back pocket. With fingers flying, she sent Colleen a text: "Need favor. Please check out 531 Fifth Avenue during your lunch hour or after work. Take pic of office and text back."

Katherine's phone rang immediately; she swiped the answer button. "Wow, talk about a quick response. Hi, Colleen!"

Colleen laughed on the other end. "What's this about?" she asked curiously.

"There's a new financial advisor in town and he said he had an office in Manhattan. It's not far from where I used to work. He has credentials that seem legit, but I have a gut feeling he's a fraud and might be ripping people off."

"I'm all over it like a cheap suit," Colleen laughed. "I'll go there at lunch. The walk will do me just fine," she said, disconnecting the call.

Katherine didn't mention that the cats also suspected something fishy regarding the loud, talkative man. Or was it just a coincidence they had destroyed the paperwork?

Later, Katherine called Mark Dunn. He didn't pick up, so she left a voice mail. An hour earlier she had sent him the pic Colleen took of Robbie's so-called Manhattan office. The photo showed an office door with a large, frosted-glass window insert. The mutual fund management firm's name was on the bottom half of the glass. But the more prominent name near the top was a Hong Kong-based party favor company managed by a George Kaplan. Katherine wondered, *Why are top money managers sharing office space?* The photo of the door raised a red flag.

In a few minutes, Mark called. He spoke hurriedly. "I've got a conference call in a few minutes. Why did you send me that picture?"

Katherine answered. "That's Robert Brentwood's New York office."

"And? What are you not telling me? I'm confused," Mark said.

"Robbie came to my house today and returned several boxes of my great aunt's belongings the museum isn't using. He told me about an investment opportunity through his New York colleagues. I gave Colleen the address on his business card and she went over there. How could a prominent mutual fund manager operate out of a seedy-looking office run by an importer of party favors?" she asked suspiciously.

Mark said dismissively, "It would make sense that Robbie would close his office since he moved out here. Maybe his colleagues work in a different office."

Katherine bit her tongue. She thought, *he never takes me seriously!* She said, annoyed, "It looks like a mail drop!"

"Look Katz, I'm having dinner with him tonight. I'll ask him — "

"Oh, Mark, don't do that. This is confidential between lawyer and client. I was just curious and want to make sure he's legit before I invest with him."

"Okay. I've got an incoming call." The phone clicked in her ear. He hung up the phone without saying good-bye.

Katherine said out loud, "Rude! Was that abrupt or what?"

Scout trotted in the room and cried, "Ma-waugh."

She picked up the Siamese and hugged her. "I love you, magic cat," she cooed. "Did you surf up the e-trading company? If so, can you figure out what stocks I need to buy?"

Scout struggled to be put down. Then she scratched her ears, crossed her eyes, and ran off to the next room.

Chapter Three

After Katherine picked up Colleen and her mum at the Indianapolis airport, she drove nine miles to a quaint restaurant in a small town the size of Erie. The restaurant was housed in a townhouse built in 1890; the couple who operated it lived upstairs. It was located across the street from a Beaux Arts-style courthouse, which filled the entire block. Parking spaces were few and far between. Katherine circled the square several times before she found one.

She apologized to her guests, "I've never seen it so busy. Last time Jake and I came here it was a virtual ghost town."

Colleen complained, "I'm starving. Quick, fast, Katz, find us a place to eat — "

Mrs. Murphy — Mum — interrupted, "And 'twould be grand to have a cup of coffee."

"Both of you are in for a treat. The restaurant I'm taking you to is fabulous. But promise me you'll go native. No lamb chops for the two of you. Today I suggest you eat what the Hoosiers eat."

"The who?" Mrs. Murphy asked, perplexed.

Colleen answered, "That's what the natives here are called. Let me guess, breaded pork tenderloin sandwiches?"

"And not to forget, the tallest, deepest, creamiest coconut cream pie on this planet."

"Okay, Mum, I get it. This is why Jake brought Katz here. They are both nuts about coconut cream pie," Colleen said with a smirk.

Katherine found a spot and parked diagonally. The trio got out and crossed the street to the mom and pop restaurant/bed & breakfast. A sign overhead announced, "Sugar Pie Inn." Colleen and Katherine took Mum's arms and escorted her through the slushy snow until they got to the restaurant entrance.

A rosy-cheeked woman greeted them, then seated them by the door. She had snow-white hair, and wore a Santa Claus hat. "Our special today is country-fried steak with mashed potatoes and brown gravy. My husband is wearing the chef hat today, and he just made a fresh batch of buttermilk biscuits." She placed menus all around. "I'll send Candy over to take your orders."

"Thanks," Katherine said.

Colleen stifled a laugh. "Sugar Pie? Candy?"

Katherine laughed. "It's a mom and sugar pop restaurant."

"Stop! I can't take it," Colleen joked.

"Mom's name is Honey," Katherine snickered. "I've got a million of 'em."

Mrs. Murphy asked, "Katz, what's sugar pie?"

"Jake said it has lots of sugar in it mixed with heavy cream."

"I might try it later," she answered.

Colleen looked around the room at the walls, which were completely covered with large photographs in faux gold plaster frames. "Did people back then ever smile?" she asked.

Mrs. Murphy piped in, "Maybe they didn't have any teeth." She then laughed at her own joke.

Katherine explained, "The owner told me her hobby is to go to antique stores to buy portraits of unusual-looking people."

"She must do a lot of antique shopping, because the walls are covered," Colleen said, then complained, "If Candy doesn't get over here quick, I'm going to die in my seat."

Candy sauntered over from a nearby customer's table and sullenly took their orders. After she left, Katherine whispered to Colleen, "She heard you. Now she's going to do something to our food."

Colleen rolled her eyes.

"How was your flight, Mum?" Katherine asked.

"After waitin' a lifetime to pass through security, our flight was late takin' off," Mrs. Murphy began. "Then the turbulence made me head spin. I'm happy to have me feet firmly planted on the ground." Mrs. Murphy's Irish brogue was much thicker than Colleen's, whose speech barely had a hint.

When the drinks arrived — iced tea for Katherine, hot tea for Colleen, and a black coffee for Mum — Mrs. Murphy pulled a silver flask from her bag. She then took out an airline size liquor bottle, and with a small plastic funnel, poured it into the flask. Pouring the amber liquid into her coffee, she said, "Nothing like a bit of Irish whisky to calm one's nerves."

Colleen threw her mother a dirty look. "Isn't it a bit early in the day to be drinkin', Mum?"

Katherine was momentarily caught off-guard. She had never seen Mrs. Murphy take a drop of alcohol, let alone a shot in her coffee.

Mrs. Murphy ignored the remark and drank her coffee with a smile.

The silence between mother and daughter was awkward. Katherine brought up the topic of the holiday fundraiser. "I've been enlisted to man a table at the annual Erie charity event. My friend Michelle Pike is in charge. I've volunteered to bake cat-shaped cookies. I was wondering if either one of you would like to contribute, as well? A percentage of the money we receive is donated to the food bank."

Colleen pouted. Mrs. Murphy sipped more of her coffee.

Katherine continued, "Mum, I thought you could sew something. Colleen, you could help me ice the cookies."

Finally, Colleen answered, "Katz, I can't imagine you baking anything."

Katherine put her hand on her hip. "Not fair. I realize I've had my share of baking disasters, but I found a wonderful recipe in one of my great aunt's cookbooks and did a trial run. The cookies turned out perfectly."

"Perrfectly," Mrs. Murphy rolled her Rs.

Colleen said, "Okay, I can ice. But I get to pick the colors."

Mrs. Murphy said, "I can sew cat cozy blankets. Katz, do you have a sewing machine?"

"There's a brand new one still in the box. I think it's got your name on it," Katherine joked.

"Gr-r-rand, I'll need several yards of fleece. Erie cats won't know what hit them." She hiccupped loudly. "Beg pardon," she said quietly.

"Great! I think it will be fun," Katherine said.

"When is it?" Colleen asked.

"Next Saturday. I forgot to ask Michelle where, but I'll find out."

"Probably at the fish fry place," Colleen said, remembering last October. "Hope they move the trucks out so there's room," she laughed. "And that they have heat."

"I was thinking of taking Abra and Scout. It could help drum up business — the iced cookies venture. Their presence could possibly increase our sales. We need to lure people over to our table. The more cookies we sell, the more money for the food bank. I could set their traveling carrier on the table."

Colleen nearly choked on her tea. "How long will that last before they start killing each other?"

Katherine laughed, knowing Colleen was referring to the move from Manhattan and how three cats in a carrier didn't work out.

"I amend that. Maybe two cat carriers."

"Whatever," Colleen said indifferently. "Katz, wouldn't it be easier to just write this organization a check? You're like a millionaire already."

"How do you know I didn't already do that?" Katherine countered, then changed the subject, "Oh, I forgot to mention, I'm having a tea later this afternoon."

Colleen said, "This is getting even richer. Katz, seriously, you're having a tea."

"Yes, and I need your help with the presentation."

"Who's coming to the tea?" Colleen asked.

"A very nice lady, in her late eighties, and her son. She knew my great aunt. I invited her over so I could get to know her, and ask questions about my great aunt. Her son is coming, too, because he's her chauffeur; she doesn't drive anymore."

Mrs. Murphy said, sneaking another shot of whiskey in her cup, "Katz, I think that's a wonderful idea."

"Just a warning! The son has a very charismatic personality with a booming voice. Colleen, he's the one whose office in Manhattan turned out to be shared with a party favor company."

"The investment banker — "

"Financial advisor," Katherine corrected.

Colleen asked, "So, is the guy a crim or not? What did Mark say about the pic I took?"

"He gave me the brush-off, as usual. The new financial advisor grew up in Erie so he's definitely part of the good ol' boy network. He's so loud and pushy, I'm surprised he's able to drum up business in this laid-back town. But apparently he's doing it because people are flocking in droves to his office."

"Uh-huh! Interesting," Colleen remarked, and then said, "If you're having a tea, we better pick up some things. Is there a market around here?"

"Great plan," Katherine agreed. "Actually there's a shop here on the square that sells tea."

Mrs. Murphy interjected, "We need to make scones to nibble on. Did you know Colleen makes the best scones?" She slurred the word, "scones."

"Yes, Mum. I will bake *something to nibble on,* but hand me that flask. That's your last nip of the day."

Reluctantly, Mrs. Murphy handed the flask to her daughter. Server Candy brought the food and announced each dish as she set down the plate. Katherine thanked her. Mother and daughter pouted and picked at their food while Katherine dove in. Later she noted her food was delicious, without comment from Colleen or her mum.

*   *   *

Back in Erie and the pink mansion, Katherine showed Mrs. Murphy to her room. Mum complained of a headache and asked to lie down a while, but to wake her an hour before the tea. Katz put her in the front turret guest room. Colleen had already run down the hall and was unpacking her carry-on suitcase. Katherine unlocked her bedroom door and the cats flew out. Scout, Abra and Iris ran down the hall, but Lilac and Abby wanted to investigate what Colleen was doing in the next room.

Katherine made a habit of locking them up whenever she left the house. Inside the room was a newly installed window alarm with a Scout-proof lock. No Russian magician or Erie nutcase would ever be able to barge in and steal one of her cats. After Iris was stolen, Katherine convinced Mark Dunn to install a state-of-the-art security system throughout the house. He was reluctant, but finally agreed.

Abby jumped on Colleen's bed and immediately dove for a sweater Colleen had just unpacked.

"Oh, no you don't," Colleen said, yanking the sweater away.

Katherine giggled, remembering how Abby had a wool fetish and loved to munch on sweaters, particularly Irish cable-knits. She became serious and asked, "Colleen, what's going on with Mum? Why was she drinking?"

Colleen sat down on the bed and gave a look of pure dejection. "Mum just found out her building is going condo. She's rented the place forever and a day. She's fit to be tied, because she doesn't want to tie up her savings in real estate."

"But the drinking part? I've never seen Mum take a drink."

"This just started. I'm at my wits end of what to do. She's taking more and more nips from that flask day in and day out. I can't believe she made it through airport security with that flask in her purse. I guess because it was empty, they allowed it. That bottle of booze she whipped out at the restaurant was from the plane. She ordered it for me while I went to the restroom. When I came back to my seat, she was putting it in her purse. She'd already had two drinks."

They both were startled when they heard a scream coming from the front guest room. Katherine and Colleen rushed down the hall to find Mrs. Murphy pointing at something on the turret floor.

"A rat!" she screamed.

Katherine hurried over to investigate but found Lilac's one-armed, one-legged toy bear. She turned to Mrs. Murphy. "Ah, don't worry, that's one of my cat's toys," she said holding it up.

Mrs. Murphy held her hand to her chest. "I thought I was dead in me bed."

Colleen said tartly, "You're probably hallucinating from the whiskey you've been drinking. Rats don't look like toy bears!"

Mrs. Murphy turned a shade of red and said, "Katz, I really need to lie down. Can you make sure none of your cats are in here so I'm not disturbed?"

"Of course," Katherine answered. She wondered where the cats were, which could be anywhere. A quick look under the bed didn't reveal any four-legged creatures. Katz assumed they had wandered downstairs or were back in Colleen's room getting into more catly mischief. "I think the coast is clear, Mum. Get some rest. I'll wake you in a bit." Katherine shut the door and whispered to Colleen, "Are you sure she's okay and it's not something else — like a medical condition?"

Colleen walked back to her room and said, "She just got a checkup. Everything is fine, but the doctor put her on blood pressure medicine."

"Maybe we should check to see if she can drink alcohol with that prescription."

"Okay."

*   *   *

Promptly at four o'clock, Robbie drove up with Lizard in the passenger seat. He parked his Lexus in front, then walked to the other side of the car to help his mother. She leaped out like a spring chicken. Robbie hardly had time to take her arm to escort her up the walk.

Mrs. Murphy was already seated in the living room, on Abby's and Iris's favorite wingback chair. She was nibbling on a scone and complaining that Colleen wasn't fast enough with the tea. Katherine glanced out the sidelight and opened the door.

"Hello!" she said cheerily.

"Oh, how lovely," Lizard said, coming in. She stopped and gave Katherine a soft look. "You look just like Orvenia when she was young. Same black hair and green eyes."

"Please join me in the living room," Katherine beamed. "Allow me to take your coat." It was then she noticed the fur wrap around Lizard's neck and shoulders. It was an old-style fur stole featuring two — very dead — fox heads. Their black glass eyes seemed to be staring at her. Momentarily taken aback, she turned to Robbie, who had already taken off his coat. He laid it over a chair.

"Katz," he boomed. "I hope you won't take offense by my being so informal. But the last time I used your hall tree, your cats attacked my coat. Ha, ha!"

Lizard broke out laughing. "Yes, he told me all about it. Here son, drape my wrap over your coat."

Katherine observed Iris peeking around the corner with a predatory glint in her sapphire blue eyes. She had zeroed in on the fox wrap.

Colleen's mum stood up and said, "I'm Mrs. Murphy, but my friends call me Maggie."

Robbie moved to the delicate Belter chair he was determined to crush and sat down, while Lizard chose the velvet loveseat.

Mrs. Murphy sat back down. "My daughter is in the kitchen makin' tea. I think she flew to India to gather the leaves," she said, amused, but with a hint of sarcasm in her voice.

Colleen came into the room holding a tray. "I heard that, Mum!" She set the tray on a marble-top coffee table.

Robbie said, eyeing Colleen, "What a lovely daughter you have, Mrs. Murphy!"

"Maggie," Mrs. Murphy corrected. "Oh, please, you'll give her a big head!"

Katherine sat down next to Lizard. Not because she wanted to be close to her guest, but it was the best vantage point in the room to observe Iris and her possible stalking of the fox wrap. She didn't trust her. She knew her. There might be trouble. She regretted not putting Iris up in her room.

"Shall I pour?" Colleen said in a refined voice worthy of *Downton Abby*.

"Yes, please," Katherine said.

"One lump or two," Colleen said to Lizard.

"Four lumps of sugar, no more, no less," Lizard said joyfully.

"None for me," Robbie said. "Ladies, would you excuse me for a moment. Katz, where is your gentleman's room?" he asked, standing up.

Katherine pointed. "Go out those pocket doors through the dining room to the kitchen, then turn left."

Robbie walked out, the wood floorboards creaking beneath his every step. Mrs. Murphy passed around the tray with the scones.

"Delicious," Lizard said. "I'll have to have this recipe."

"It's a mix," Colleen said and then countered, "Of course, I'll write it out for you."

They heard loud voices from the kitchen.

Katherine asked Colleen, "Who's out there?"

"Cokey just stopped by to pick up that defective microwave."

"Does anyone want cream in their tea?" Katherine asked, making an excuse. "I'll go to the kitchen and get some," she said, getting up.

"Who needs cream when I've got something better," Mum said, pulling out her silver flask.

Lizard said, "Gimme a hit, too! Back in the day, I used to carry one in my stocking."

"Mum," Colleen scolded. "You took that out of my bag!"

Katherine stopped outside the kitchen door, and felt a little embarrassed about eavesdropping. Cokey sounded angry. Very angry. Robbie was trying to assure him about something, speaking in a calming voice.

"You better wipe that shit-eatin' grin off your face before I knock your lights out," Cokey threatened. "I *want* my money back," he demanded. "I haven't seen any returns on my investment like you promised."

"You must be patient. This mutual fund makes distributions every three months. You haven't given it enough time," Robbie said in a quiet voice.

"Yes, I have. That's my kids' college fund that your fancy friends in New York are playing with. I'll be by your office later to sign whatever I need to sign and get *out* of that fund. Got it? Have the papers ready!" Cokey stormed out of the room. Katherine could hear him opening and slamming the door to the back stairs to the basement. She hurried to the living room — not wanting Robbie to see her — and sat back down. Her heart sank when she heard Cokey say he had invested his children's college fund.

Lizard was telling a story to Mrs. Murphy.

"Where's the cream?" Colleen whispered.

"Oh, I changed my mind."

Lizard continued and said to Katherine, "Your great aunt was quite the lady, but did you know she had a lover?"

Robbie came back into the room and admonished, "Mother, really. Katherine doesn't want to hear that."

"No, actually I do." Katherine leaned closer to Lizard to hear more.

"Inquiring minds . . ." Colleen encouraged.

"He was her chauffeur for a number of years. Everyone in town knew what was going on."

"What happened to him?" Katherine asked.

"He died in the Battle of the Bulge — 1944, I believe. Orvenia was devastated."

"How tragic," Katherine said.

Lizard continued. "War hasn't been kind to Orvenia or me. My husband — Robbie's father — died in the Vietnam War. We'd only been married a few years. Robbie was a surprise baby. I was thirty-nine when I had him."

Doing the math in her head, Katherine blurted, "Was Robbie's dad a general?"

Lizard laughed. "He was a second lieutenant. You see, Katz, I preferred younger men. I was fourteen years older than Robert, Senior."

Katherine thought, *Maybe son takes after his mother. Preferring younger partners.*

Colleen's eyes suddenly widened as she looked past the house guests. She moved forward in her chair and began making hand gestures to Katherine. First, she made cat ears with her fingers, then the sign of pulling. She pointed at the chair where the Brentwoods had placed their coats. No one but Katherine noticed her pantomime.

Katherine saw the fox wrap slowly slide off the chair. Scout and Abra were dragging it out of the room. She got up and quickly moved over to the site, but it was too late. Scout and Abra had the wrap in the atrium and were attacking the fox heads. Iris joined in. A wrestling match ensued. It wasn't clear to whom the kill belonged. And then snarls, hissing and growling began.

"Give it to me," Katherine demanded. Scout and Abra both had the wrap in their teeth — tearing at it like a tug-of-war. "Now," she said adamantly. She snatched the wrap away from the rowdy cats and slowly walked back into the living room. She felt all eyes upon her.

"I'm so sorry," she apologized to Lizard. She handed her the disheveled wrap.

Robbie and Colleen burst out laughing.

Lizard said, "Don't worry, my dear. I've had that wrap forever and it has survived many battles."

Robbie glanced at his mother with a *what did that mean* expression.

"Oh, a plague of moths one season!" Lizard laughed, then announced, "Son, I've grown very tired. I think it's time to say thank you and good bye to our fine hosts."

Robbie walked over and took his mother by the hand. He helped her with her coat and ceremoniously wrapped the fur wrap around her neck. Walking out of the mansion, Lizard said to Katherine. "We'll keep in touch. There is so much more I can tell you about your great aunt." She winked and then left with her surprisingly quiet but attentive son.

Before closing the door, Katherine did a quick look-see up and down Lincoln Street to make sure that PETA activists weren't poised to launch a paint bomb attack on the unsuspecting couple. The street was empty. "Close call," Katherine sighed and shut the door.

Colleen said to her mum, "You shouldn't have given her that booze! No wonder she was tired."

*   *   *

The pink mansion's back office and kitchen became the staging ground for the production of items to be sold at the fundraising event on the following Saturday. Colleen's mum sat in front of a sewing machine, racing through yet another cat cozy blanket to sell at the Erie holiday event. Katherine and Colleen were in the kitchen icing cookies in the shape of cats —mostly headless.

Katherine complained, "I don't understand how this happened. Their heads were intact when I put them in the oven."

"I think we can just use icing to join them — like a decorative cat collar," Colleen said with a grin.

"How many more do we have to bake?" Katherine said counting them. "We've got four dozen right now, minus the ones you ate."

"Me! I only ate the tailless ones," Colleen argued.

Mrs. Murphy called into the room, "Hey, the two of you! I could use some help."

Colleen began laughing. She couldn't stop. She sat back on the aluminum chair, tipped her head back and laughed more. "Katz, this is a comedy act. Who will buy a headless cat cookie?"

"I don't know, but maybe we should put more flour in the next batch," Katz said, determined to make the venture a success. Then she noticed her friend was using green icing to frost the cookies. "Carrot top, there's no such thing as a green cat."

"Well, missy, I remember you saying I had creative license. So, bite the bullet. I choose the colors."

Mrs. Murphy yelled in, "Stop fussin', you two. Katz, one of your cats is doin' something to your computer."

Katherine dried her hands on her apron, and with Colleen, sprinted into the office.

"What are you talking about?" Katherine asked. "I don't see a cat."

"There was one a second ago. I was sewin' to beat the band when I heard a clickin' sound. I turned around and saw one of your cats sittin' on the chair, pawin' the mouse thing."

"Which one?" Katherine asked eagerly, thinking maybe she'd finally find out which feline was surfing the web.

"Mum, which one?" Colleen seconded.

Mrs. Murphy shrugged. "How am I supposed to know? It was a cat. I've got me readin' glasses on. I'm as blind as a bat with distances."

"Okay, what color was the cat?" Katz prodded.

"Gray, I think."

Katz and Colleen shared inquisitive glances. "Lilac? It's possible," Colleen noted. "I've seen her up here before."

Katherine countered, "I've seen *all* of them up here before. This isn't evidence."

Looking at the monitor, Colleen said, "This doesn't make any sense. Why would she surf up a movie review of *Gosford Park*. That's an old movie."

Katherine hurried over and glanced at the screen. "The movie's not that old," and then to

Mum, "No worries. My cats are always stepping on the mouse and conjuring up something."

Mrs. Murphy answered, "I just didn't want any harm to come to your stuff. Now I've got seven more of these blasted things to sew. My eyes are crossed, and I'm ready to hit me bed for a nap."

Katherine and Colleen ignored her. "Maybe we should Netflix the movie and watch it tonight. It's a Robert Altman film."

"I've seen it," Colleen said. "I'll give you a short review: weekend party at an upper-class estate in 1932. Head of the household is murdered. The police are baffled by whodunit."

Katherine laughed, "Cheater! You just read the review. That's what it says."

"Girls!" Mrs. Murphy said. "Snap out of it! Colleen, you can cut, and Katz can pin. Get busy!"

Colleen winked, then said to her mum. "All right, hand me the scissors."

Katherine said, "Let me finish in the kitchen, then I'll be right back." When she walked in the room, two very guilty brown-masked Siamese flew out. Abra was clutching a cookie in her jaws. Scout had one too." "Dammit!" she said, turning the oven off and then chasing after the feline thieves.

Mrs. Murphy and Colleen were laughing. Colleen pointed, "They went that way."

The front doorbell rang its festive greeting.

"I'll get it," Katherine said, dashing out of the room.

Opening the door, Katherine saw a woman in her twenties with long, blond hair and blue eyes. She was very sun-tanned and had a beautiful smile.

"Hi, I'm Emily," the girl said.

"Robbie called and said you were coming. I'll show you the living room, where the portraits are."

Emily brought in a large hard-shell camera case and a tripod. Lilac and Abby seemed to be very interested and followed them into the living room.

Katherine said, "If you need anything, I'm in the back room."

It had only been a few minutes when Emily came back and said to Katherine, "I can't get a good shot of your great uncle's portrait."

"Why's that?" Katherine asked.

"Your cat — the one with the gray face and ears — waits for me to set up the shot, then zooms up to the fireplace mantel and pushes the portrait so it's crooked."

Colleen put her hand over her mouth and suppressed a giggle.

Katherine moved away from the cozy she was pinning and followed Emily back to the living room. Emily's camera case was turned upside down, with various lenses and gadgets spilling out on the floor. Lilac and Abby sat on their window valance perch, eyeing the two humans with looks of complete innocence on their faces. Katherine knew better. One of them had rifled the case.

Katherine explained, "I'm sorry, but my cat is too high for me to get without setting up a ladder. Maybe if I stay in the room you can get your shot. If it looks like she's going to jump down, I'll try to distract her."

Emily stooped down and righted the camera case. She began shoving the spilled items back into it. There was something missing, because she crawled around the floor looking under furniture.

"Has something gone missing?" Katherine asked.

"Ah, yes," Emily said, getting up. "It's not important. I think maybe I'd left it at home, and it wasn't in the case after all."

"Just a second. My cats sometimes take things and hide them in their favorite chair. Let me look." Katherine fell to her knees and felt inside the wingback chair. Lilac and Abby craned their necks to see. "I'm not finding anything. If something turns up, I'll give you a call."

Emily gave a quick worried look, then looked at her camera's viewing screen and took the shot without any more shenanigans from Lilac. When finished, she said, "I hope you'll be pleased with what Robbie has done with your family's display. It's super cool."

"I can't wait to see it. Are you going to attend the museum opening?"

"Yes, of course, as Robbie's date. Actually, if you can keep a secret, I think he's going to announce our engagement. But look surprised when he does," Emily said happily.

"Where did you two meet?"

"In Hawaii! My mom is a marine biologist and works in Chicago. She had a meeting in Hawaii and took me along. I'm so glad I went because at a cocktail party, I met Robbie. It was love at first sight. I thought he was so funny. He talked me into moving to Indiana."

Katherine wondered how Emily got a word in edgewise to even flirt with the loquacious Robbie, who was twice her age. Katherine said, "Congratulations. I wish the both of you much happiness."

After Emily finished putting her camera away, Katherine led her to the door. Scout walked in front of them and arched her back. Her fur was bristled and she gave a low growl. Then, she hopped up and down like a Halloween cat.

"Scout, come here sweetie," Katherine said, trying to pick up the cat, but she sped off to the dining room.

"That cat is really scary!" Emily said guardedly.

"I'm so sorry. I don't know what got into her . . . " Katherine suddenly felt a premonition that something wasn't quite right. She worried for Emily. Opening the door, she said, "Be careful out there. The roads can be pretty slippery with all this snow."

"It was awesome to meet you. I'll see you at the opening." Emily smiled and walked to her car.

Katherine closed the door and turned to find Scout. She called her name several times, but only Abra came. The Siamese was licking her chops. A small glob of green icing was on her lip. "Hey, my sweet girl. I hope you didn't eat the entire cookie. Where's your sister?" Katherine picked her up and wiped off the icing. She held her for a moment.

"Raw," Abra cried uneasily. She carried her to the kitchen where Scout was lapping up a drink of water. She set Abra down next to Scout.

"Magic cat, is something going to happen to Emily?"

Scout continued drinking, then looked up with a drop of water on her nose. "Ma-waugh," she cried evasively.

"Does that mean yes or no?"

Scout sat up and stood tall on the ceramic-tiled floor. With the grace of a ballerina, she lifted her leg and started cleaning the inside of her toes. Her eyes were deliberately crossed, in a deranged look. She seemed to enjoy darting her pink tongue in and out of her claws.

"Okay, I take that as a no," Katherine said, walking into the office to resume her sewing endeavor.

Scout continued washing.

Chapter Four

Early Saturday morning, Jake drove to the pink mansion to help Katz, Colleen and Mrs. Murphy move their wares to the Erie annual holiday fundraiser. He drove his dad's pickup truck with the extended cab. On Katherine's lap, he placed the cat carrier containing a very happy Siamese. Lilac cried with excitement, knowing she was about to have an adventure. Scout, Abra, Iris and Abby looked outside the parlor window with great disdain. They wanted to go, too, but handling five hyperactive cats was too much. Arriving at the armory, the four got out of the truck and walked to the art deco style building. Jake carried the cat carrier.

Katherine admired, "I love the yellow glazed tiles on the façade and the tiled roof. When was it built?"

Jake answered, "1931. It was financed by WPA funds. It recently received a total rehab. Back in the nineties, it was a complete dump."

Walking inside, the group removed their coats and hung them on hooks outside the large, open room. Inside, a bank of tables was set up on a gleaming floor made of geometric-patterned tiles. The tall ceiling was curved, exposing the original roof trusses. The room was lined with two-story windows, which admitted a lot of light.

Jake continued, "This used to be the drill hall where troops were trained, but now it's used by the town for dances, weddings and seasonal events."

Michelle Pike bustled over, "Katz, hey!" She extended her hand to Mrs. Murphy, "You must be Colleen's mom. "I'm Michelle. I'm so pleased to meet you. Hi, Colleen. Hope you're enjoying your visit. Hey, Jake. Is this the cat?" she said, peering in and admiring Lilac.

"Me-yowl" was Lilac's loud reply.

"Follow me, gang," she directed. "I'll show you where your table is."

The group followed Michelle. Each table was decorated with a holiday-themed tablecloth. Katherine admired the many vendors displaying their wares: homemade candles, soaps, and decorated Christmas ornaments.

Katherine's table was at the end of the row. She placed her box of cookies on top, while Mrs. Murphy spread out her cat cozy blankets. Jake set the cat carrier in the middle. Colleen complained there wasn't a third chair, so she and Michelle went off to look for one. Mrs. Murphy sat down and opened the money box.

In the center of the large room, against one of the long walls, was a platform/stage with a microphone stand. In front was an elaborately decorated long table with a red velvet skirt. It was covered with cakes — every conceivable kind of fancy cake. Katherine moved over to it. Her eyes grew big as they darted from cake to cake, examining each with awe.

On the table was a three-tiered coconut cake, a log cabin made from Twinkies, a Santa Claus sheet cake, a snowman covered with shredded coconut, several chocolate cakes, and a detailed Victorian Queen Anne gingerbread house iced with pink frosting.

Jake came over. "That looks like your house."

Katherine scrutinized it. "The detailing is very good, but I'm not liking the grim reaper figurine in the front door."

"You're kidding me," Jake said looking. When he saw it, he chuckled. "Looks like something from a Halloween miniature set."

Katherine drummed her fingers on the table. "The murder house!" She gazed around the room and when she didn't see anyone looking, she removed a graham cracker door, put the figurine inside, and then put the door back. "Solved," she giggled.

"You're lucky a cake Nazi didn't see you, or you'd be in a heap of trouble," Jake advised, then asked, "What do you think of this cake?" He pointed at a giant cone of chocolate set on a bank of red icing.

"It looks like a volcano. It's even got chocolate spouting out of the top of it."

Jake smiled. "That's my mom's cake. It's her famous volcano cake. She bakes one every year. That's an official chocolate pump. Liquid magma."

Katherine said, "Cool! I don't see any prices on these cakes."

"People come from miles around to bid on them. This is how the event makes most of its money."

"Bid?" Katherine questioned. "I don't get it."

"It's a cake auction! There's even an auctioneer. It starts promptly at noon. Word of advice — things could get ugly, but in a good way," Jake grinned. "Hey listen, sweet pea, I'm off now. I'll be back at high noon."

"Seriously, you're coming back for the cake auction?" Katherine asked, surprised.

"I wouldn't miss it for the world. Because," he began, then lowered his voice. "See that flowerpot behind the volcano?"

"Yeah?"

"Inside that ordinary clay pot is the most *delicious* white chocolate cake you've ever tasted."

Katherine rolled her eyes and pinched him affectionately on the arm. "Okay, I won't tell anyone you're going to bid on that cake. But here's a little ditty about Jack and Diane. I know who made *said* cake."

"Oh, really?" he asked. "And who baked *said* cake?"

"That's for me to know and you to find out."

"Okay, savvy girl, I look forward to finding out. See you later," Jake said, leaving, enjoying the playful banter. Katherine followed him with her eyes and saw him stop and talk to his mother, Cora, who was standing in the entryway. Jake saw Katz looking, so he pointed at his mom. Katherine waved. Cora waved back.

One of the Sanders boys — the one with the irritating hyena laugh — walked in. Bobby took the shortest route to the cake registration table where there were two chairs but no occupants. Elizabeth "Lizard" Brentwood slowly walked to the table and took her seat. Son Robbie took the second chair. A colorful banner attached to the table announced "Cake Auction 2014."

Bobby Sanders was carrying some sort of sheet cake. He carefully set it down on the table and began to fill out an entry form. Katherine moved over to look at the cake. She smiled at Lizard and Robbie.

The cake depicted a Hawaiian hula dancer with a blue-iced cupcake bra. Black Twizzlers formed the straps and the grass hula skirt was made from red shoe-string licorice. A Hershey's chocolate kiss was in the dancer's belly button.

Cora stormed over and looked aghast at the cake. "Lizard, he can't enter that cake. It's indecent," she said indignantly.

Lizard said in her raspy voice, "Now Cora, Mr. Sanders can and will enter this cake."

"Yeah, lady," Bobby said, and then laughed loudly.

Cora's face reddened. She turned brusquely on her heels and stomped out of the room.

Lizard leaned over and said to Bobby, "I think your cake is a hoot! Wouldn't it be great if your cake made the most money for the charity?"

Bobby broke out into a big smile and acted as if he'd never been praised for anything in his entire life. "Thank ya, Ma'am," he said as he left.

Katherine strolled back to her assigned table and stayed there until the cake auction began. She never saw Cora again, so she assumed she'd left. It was okay by her. Jake's mother, true to her character, had given her the cold shoulder and had not even spoken to her.

"What was that about?" Colleen asked.

Katherine chuckled. "One of the Sanders boys entered an X-rated cake. Well, maybe not X-rated, but Jake's mom thought so."

Colleen rushed over to see the cake and then started laughing. Returning she said, "Hilarious!"

Cokey, Margie and their two kids, Tommy and Shelly, walked in. They each carried a barn sash window under their arms. Shelly struggled with hers. Margie's table was set up next to Katherine's.

"Hey, you guys," Margie said to the group. "Wait until you see what I've done with these old barn windows. I found them on the street and thought it was a shame to just throw them away." Margie, an ace at restoring old buildings, was also very adept at reclaiming ancient items and giving them a second chance.

Mrs. Murphy, Colleen and Katherine checked them out. On the glass part of the sash, Margie had painted festive holiday scenes. She had attached LED lights to make the snow glisten. The barn windows instantly became a big hit as people came over to admire them. Mrs. Murphy bought the first one, and later lamented she didn't know how she was going to get it on the plane when she flew home. Cokey and Tommy left the armory and brought in more barn windows.

A crowd had grown around Katherine's table. Everyone wanted to see the lilac-point Siamese. Lilac was in her element. She'd nuzzled up to the metal cat grate at every passerby who stopped to admire her. Each time, she emitted an ear-splitting Siamese ME-YOWL, which after a while was almost deafening.

A thirty-something man with black hair and light blue eyes came over. He was carrying a digital camera. "Hi, I'm Russell. Russell Krow. I'm a reporter for the *Erie Herald.*"

"Spelled like the Australian actor?" Colleen asked.

"No, we spell our last names differently." He looked at Katherine. "You have to be Orvenia Colfax's great niece, because you look just like her when she was younger."

"Yes, but how do you know what she looked like?" Katherine asked.

He smiled, showing perfect teeth. "I just came from the museum. I took several shots of the

Colfax displays. Would it be okay if I took a pic of all of you sitting behind the table?"

Katherine asked Colleen and Mum if it would be okay. "Sure, I haven't had me picture in the newspaper lately," Mrs. Murphy said.

"No problem," Colleen answered.

The three leaned in with Lilac's carrier still on the middle of the table.

The newspaper reporter snapped a pic. He asked them for their names, which he wrote on an index card, then zeroed in on Katherine. "I'd be honored to interview you . . . for the paper, of course. Could I take you to dinner some evening? Here's my card," he said, extracting one from the inside of his jacket and handing it to her.

"Better yet, why don't I call you and arrange a time for you to meet me for lunch," Katherine suggested.

"Great," he said, looking directly into her eyes. He smiled and left.

Colleen whispered, "Was he hitting on you, or what? What's with that lunch comment?"

"Mom used to say, 'lunch is for friends, dinner is for lovers.'"

Colleen rolled her eyes. "Whatever! You've got to admit he was hot."

"Hotter eye candy than Daryl?"

"I wouldn't go that far. What's with these Indiana men anyway? Most of them are gorgeous hunks."

Several potential buyers came to the table and began looking through Mrs. Murphy's cozy blankets. They began to sell like hotcakes, but the cookies were a disaster. No one wanted them. Even with Lilac striking a Hollywood pose in her carrier, Katz hadn't sold a single green-iced cat cookie.

Colleen sensed her friend's disappointment and grabbed a cookie. "Don't feel bad, Katz. They're really tasty. Give it time."

The morning wore on. It was getting close to noon. A boisterous crowd of ball-capped men had grouped in front of the cake table. Jake assumed his position in front of the white chocolate flowerpot cake. He caught Katherine's eye and winked.

Colleen observed, "This is a new experience for me. I've never seen men interested in a bake sale."

"Me, either," Katherine said, and then laughed, "Colleen, we've never been to a bake sale before, so how would we know."

Shelly and Tommy were getting fidgety. Shelly went over to the cake table for the twentieth time and each time came back giggling. "Mommy, the hula dancer has boobies." Margie would hush her each time, but to no avail. Tommy was clearly the more bored of the two. He kept asking Katherine if he could pet Lilac. "Katz, please? Can I hold her? She looks lonely in her cage. She wants to come out," the twelve-year-old boy pleaded.

Margie admonished, "Stop whining! It's driving your mother nuts."

Katherine reluctantly gave in. "I guess so, but only if I put her harness on. I don't want her to get loose." She opened the door and brought Lilac out and sat her on the table. Katherine placed the harness on the Siamese, snapped the buckle, and then attached a short leash. She then handed the lilac-point to Tommy.

"Ahhh," Tommy cooed. "You're such a cutie."

"Owl," Lilac cried quietly. The Siamese was hoarse from me-yowling. Her blue eyes crossed with joy.

"I want to hold her," Shelly said eagerly. "It's my turn. Let me hold her."

Then a large, loud man stepped up onto the platform and grasped the mike. Robbie said in his typical booming voice, "Welcome, folks! I'm today's auctioneer, so let's make some money for the Erie Food Bank." In his right hand he held a bugle. As he tipped it back, Katherine lunged for Lilac. *Loud noises freak Lilac out. Loud noises make Lilac crazy. Loud noises make Lilac run.*

Katherine was too late. As Robbie blew on the bugle, Lilac jumped from Tommy's arms and began leaping from table to table, leaving a wake of tumbled wares — candles, soaps, and ribbon-tied bags of potpourri —scattered all over the floor. Katherine made a mad dash for her, but Lilac was too fast. At the end of the tabled row, close to the entryway, Lilac stopped abruptly, turned and ran back. Margie, Mrs. Murphy, and Colleen tried to catch the fleeing cat. Lilac tried to get inside the carrier, but the door was closed. Robbie kept blowing the bugle. Finally, Lilac jumped on top of the carrier and sat there for a split-second as if she were contemplating her next move.

"Stay, Lilac," Katherine said, inching closer to snatch her. She could see Jake in the ball-cap crowd rushing over to help her. But he was also too late.

In what seemed to be one fluid motion, Lilac launched off the carrier, soared through the air, hit the cake table, and slid into the volcano cake. It immediately exploded with liquid chocolate squirting everywhere. Some of the chocolate hit Robbie.

"Can someone bring me a towel?" he yelled over the mike.

"My cake," Cora said, reappearing out of nowhere. She looked like she was going to faint.

When Lilac tramped on the hula dancer, the cupcake bra flew into the crowd. She then stomped on the log cabin Twinkie cake like a feline Godzilla. She was about to capsize the pink iced gingerbread house, when Jake caught her. He held her in his arms and spoke softly to her. "I'll get you out of here, baby girl."

The *Erie Herald* reporter — Russell Krow — was taking pictures in a rapid-fire, machine-gun fashion. Katherine could only imagine what the front page of tomorrow's newspaper would look like.

Michelle ran over with a roll of paper towels. She had one hand covering her mouth to refrain from laughing. Katherine shook her head in amused disbelief, yanked several towels off, and began wiping the icing off Lilac's paws.

Colleen had collapsed in her chair. She was fanning herself with her hand and laughing hysterically. Mrs. Murphy smirked and took a shot of something from her flask. Jake grabbed the carrier, put Lilac inside, and with Katherine escaped to the door. The crowd opened up for them — a few of them having disappointed looks on their faces, except for Tommy's school friends at the back, who were laughing rowdily.

Once out of the armory, Katherine said, "I can take her home. You go back and bid on your flowerpot cake."

Jake grinned and kissed her on the cheek. "Okay, I'll see you when you come back." He handed her his dad's truck keys.

As Katherine drove the feline Godzilla home, she said, "What were you thinking? Capsizing Jake's mom-from-hell's cake? *You didn't!*"

Lilac was sitting serenely inside the carrier, licking the remaining icing off her paws. Once inside the mansion, four felines surrounded the carrier. Katherine opened it and Lilac flew out, taking four or five stairs at a time, "owling" the entire way upstairs. Katherine burst out laughing and then returned to the armory. The auction was finished. Jake proudly held the flowerpot cake.

Katherine asked, "How much did it go for?"

"Forty bucks. That dang Frank from the diner was bidding against me."

Katherine grinned. "Oh, how sweet! That was Frank's mom's cake. She just broke her hip. Michelle said that although she wasn't able to come, she was still able to bake it with her home health aide. Adorable!"

The cake auction was the grand finale of the holiday fundraiser. Katherine boxed up the remaining cat cookies, which was all of them, except for the ones that Colleen, Tommy and Shelly had eaten. Mrs. Murphy had sold every one of her cat cozies and had taken orders for more. She said she could make them at home and mail them. Margie was also successful. Only Katz had a box to carry home.

On the way out, one of the vendors approached Katherine and was annoyed because Lilac had broken several candles. He threatened to talk to the board about not allowing pets the next year. Katherine apologized and wrote a check for the damages. She made a mental note to ask the board about the cost of the damaged cakes so she could write a check for those, as well.

Jake drove Katherine, Colleen, and Mrs. Murphy back to the mansion, then headed over to his parents' house. Mrs. Murphy excused herself to take a nap, while Katherine and Colleen went to the kitchen for some tea.

Abby hissed at Lilac every time she got near her.

"What's that all about?" Colleen asked.

"Who knows?" Katherine shrugged. "Maybe Abby is jealous because she didn't get to go."

"Two catzillas would have been hilarious," Colleen offered. "What time is the shindig tonight?"

"You mean the grand opening of the Erie Historical Museum, by invitation only?" Katherine said in a fake TV-announcer voice. "Jake is my escort. I really want to look my best for the event. He's picking me up at seven. That gives me plenty of time to get ready. I've already laid out my clothes on great aunt Orvenia's bed. I bought the sweetest

black cocktail dress."

Colleen asked, "Was that a good idea?"

"What? Asking Jake to be my escort?"
Katherine asked quizzically.

"No, not that. I meant, was that a good idea,
laying out your new dress, considering that your cats
chew on clothes?"

"Oh, no problem. I shut the door."

Colleen filled the tea pot and put it on the
stove. "Later, send me a selfie of the two of you.
Daryl's picking Mum and me up at five. He's taking
us to meet his parents — "

"Oh, really. Meet the parents?" Katherine
interrupted.

Colleen frowned. "I'm a nervous wreck.
What if they don't like me?"

"Just be yourself."

"Katz, I don't mean to be *mean*, but you're yourself around Jake's mom, and she acts like she can't stand you."

"Oh, so you noticed. She could have at least come over and said hello, but that's her problem. I'm dating Jake, not Cora." Changing the subject, she said facetiously, "Want a cookie to go with your tea?"

"I ate too many. I feel sick. Now I have to eat dinner with Daryl. How am I going to pull that off?"

"You'll be fine. Just stop worrying." Katherine glanced at her watch and stood up. "Don't have time for tea. I've got to get a move on if I'm going to make my hair appointment. I'm getting the works: hair, nails, and makeup."

"Okay, see you later. If I'm not here when you get home, I hope you have a wonderful time."

"Oh, Colleen, can you do me a big favor? Can you feed the cats before you leave? They're used to eating dinner at five."

Colleen scrunched up her nose. "Okay, just point out the food."

"Super, it's on the counter! Give them each a small can. They like eating in here. Thanks so much." She grabbed her bag and hurried out of the mansion.

Chapter Five

When Katherine returned to the pink mansion, the cats hardly recognized her. The hair stylist had cut wispy bangs, which emphasized her large green eyes. A cosmetic artist applied makeup she'd never dream of choosing herself, but as she looked in the salon mirror, she broke out in a wide smile. She wondered how Jake would react when he saw her. With her short black hair styled, her nails painted a rich burgundy, and a Hollywood-worthy makeover, she couldn't wait to put on the short cocktail dress.

Walking in the atrium, the cats greeted her at the foot of the stairs. They eyed her suspiciously. Iris danced in and out of her legs and nearly tripped her several times.

"Miss Siam," Katherine scolded. "Stop trying to kill me."

"Yowl," Iris sassed.

Katherine began climbing the stairs. Scout and Abra had already gone ahead. Several times, they stopped and turned around to look at the alien, who looked like their person, but smelled differently. Abra turned up her lips in apparent disgust. Scout hissed.

"Okay, that's it! It's me," Katherine said. "I'm trying to look good for the big event, but you fur kids don't seem to approve."

At the top of the stairs, Katherine turned left to go into her great aunt's former bedroom and was startled to see the door open — wide open. She had specifically shut the door so the cats wouldn't go into the room.

"Scout," she accused. "I *know* you opened it."

Scout and Abra turned on their heels and ran down the stairs. "Ma-waugh," Scout cried defensively.

Rushing through the doorway, Katherine immediately realized her mistake in laying out the dress. There, on the bed, was her sexy black cocktail dress — for the event of the season — completely covered with cat hair.

"Oh, no. You didn't!" she exclaimed. In shock, she stared at the disaster for a moment, then moved her attention to Lilac and Abby who sat on their haunches at the foot of the bed.

"Proud of yourselves?" she asked the guilty-looking cats.

Abby hiccupped. "Chirp!" she cried brightly.

Immediately, Katherine remembered a similar scene where Abby had eaten a hole in Colleen's Irish cable-knit sweater. "Oh, no," she said, quickly picking up the dress and examining it. Sure enough Abby had chewed a small hole, but fortunately it was on the side hem. She didn't think it would be noticed, especially if she wore her new Gucci evening pumps with the four inch heel. The dress and the shoes had cost a small chunk of change, but Katherine told herself they were her reward for being frugal ever since she'd moved to Erie. After all, she had just deposited five million dollars in the bank; she was entitled to a treat.

Frantically, she searched upstairs for a sticky tape lint remover, to no avail. The phone in the atrium rang. She rushed downstairs to answer it.

"Hello!" she answered, slightly out of breath.

Margie asked, "Hey, kiddo, what are you wearing? I'm stuck in my closet and I can't find a thing to wear. The kids are no help. Shelly wants me to wear a rhinestone denim skirt with a western blouse, and Tommy suggested I go in my work clothes."

"Whatever you pick, Margie, I'm sure it will be fine. I've got a bit of a problem over here. I laid out my dress and the cats decided to use it as their cozy bed."

Margie laughed loudly over the phone. "Please don't tell me it was black."

"Afraid so."

"What time is Jake picking you up?"

"Around seven. The invitation said there'd be a cocktail hour — an open bar with an appetizer buffet. Is Cokey wearing a suit and tie?"

"That would be the day! Actually, Katz, he decided not to go."

"Why?" Katherine asked, somewhat shocked. *This was Margie's big night*, she thought. *Why would her husband not want to be there for her?* It was Margie's historical reconstruction of the old town library, built in the 1870s, which saved the day when the Historical Society funds were stolen by Frank and Beatrice Baker, and were never recovered. Without the money, a new museum building couldn't be erected. Margie suggested the old library as the perfect site. And the town agreed.

"He's worried about the kids staying alone, especially at night."

"I understand. If I were a parent, I'd do the same thing. Listen, do you want Jake and me to pick you up?"

"Sure," Margie said appreciatively. "That's really the main reason why I called. Only if it's no trouble."

"Of course not. We'll see you a little after seven."

"Thanks, kiddo," Margie said, hanging up.

Scout and Abra were on the curio cabinet. Abra was standing on her hind legs, sniffing the air. She had her paws on Katherine's shoulders.

"Okay, Miss Hocus Pocus, I get the part where you think I stink."

Scout leaned over the cabinet and pawed the handle. Katherine opened the drawer and found the sticky tape roller. "Smart girl," she praised, petting Scout on the head. Scout backed up and ceremoniously knocked the phone receiver off the house phone.

"Cats!" Katherine said out loud. "And to think I have five of them," she muttered.

Katherine returned upstairs to try to rescue the dress. It was impossible to remove all the cat hairs, so she did a once over with the vacuum cleaner nozzle. Satisfied she wouldn't look like a human hairball, she hurriedly put the dress on.

Glancing at her watch, she realized it was a little before seven, and Jake would be there any minute. Grabbing her evening bag, she headed for the front door.

Looking out the sidelight window, she saw Jake getting out of a classic blue Dodge Charger. He looked like a male model from GQ magazine. He wore a black suit with a crisp white dress shirt, which was unbuttoned at the collar. Katherine stared in awe as he walked up the steps, and she opened the door. It was then she noticed he was carrying a long-stem red rose.

She smiled. "Come in before you freeze to death."

"For you," he said, handing her the flower.

She closed the door. "How sweet."

Jake was silent for a moment. "You look absolutely beautiful." He gathered her in his arms and whispered, "I love you."

Katherine's eyes grew wide. She was startled to hear the words because he had never said them before. She basked in the warm glow of the sound. She took his face in her hands and looked at him lovingly. "I love you, too."

"Me-yowl," Lilac shrieked at the top of her Siamese lungs. She reached up to Jake to be held.

Jake picked up the lilac-point and kissed her on the nose. "Okay, I love you, too, Catzilla."

Katherine giggled. "Now you need the lint roller." She started to move away, but Jake stopped her.

"No need. What's a few cat hairs?" He winked.

Holding the rose, Katherine said, "I'll put this out of reach of the cats. Lilac likes to eat rose petals, and Abby would probably eat the entire stalk — thorns and all."

She was gone for a moment. When she came back, Jake was sitting on the floor, petting Abby and Lilac. "Where are the other kids?" he asked.

"Plastered on top of the register in the kitchen. Oh, before I forget, Margie needs a ride."

"Yep, Cokey just called me. He gave me his lame excuse about why he wasn't going. I think he suffers from 'suit' shock. Let's head on out and pick her up."

As Katherine locked the door, Jake asked, "Who's coming to this bash?"

"Mark Dunn said he worked on the invitation list. He said the mayor and his wife will be there. The doctor and her husband. I met them when I first visited Indiana. Members of the Society, and the principals from the Erie high school and elementary schools. Also, the new head of the library, whoever that is. Did you know Robbie Brentwood is the volunteer museum curator?"

"Ye, gods, him again," Jake commented with a face. "What is he? Like the jack of all trades?"

Katherine poked him on the arm.

Jake ushered Katherine down the sidewalk to the car.

Katherine asked, "Where's the Jeep?"

"Oh, I save the Charger for special occasions," he said in a teasing tone.

"Good to know," Katherine said. "Any more surprises for me?"

Jake answered evasively, "That's for me to know, and you to find out."

"What a minute," she said, looking at him with amused wonder. "That's my line."

"Actually, it's my dad's *muscle* car. Dad insisted. He said I *couldn't* pick you up in the Jeep. Now that Margie's coming with us, I'm glad I said yes."

As Katherine was getting in, two of the Sanders boys slowly drove by in their beat-up pickup truck, eyeing Katherine. Bobby, with the mullet, lowered his window and blew a loud wolf whistle.

"Hey, guys! Move on down the road." Jake threw them a serious look.

"Hey, Ms. Kendall, you owe me money for my cake." Before Katherine could answer, he peeled out and raced down the street.

Jake got in. "Sorry about that. Sam Sanders needs to teach his boys some manners."

"I really *do* owe him money for the cake."

"Are you kidding me? Even without the hula dancer boobs, that cake sold for fifty bucks."

Katherine brought up her hand to smother a laugh. "Which cake made the most money?"

"The pink gingerbread house sold for a hundred bucks."

"No way! I know a cake in Manhattan can cost a hundred bucks, but one selling for that in Erie? Amazing. Who won the bid?"

"The mayor's wife, Melody. It was quite a bidding war. Wish you could have seen it. Robbie wanted it, too."

"Oh, no!" Katherine exclaimed. "Should we warn her about the grim reaper figurine I put inside the house? She might break a tooth."

Jake laughed, "Thinkin' so." He turned the ignition key and the Charger's big engine roared to life. The sound of the muscle car idling could almost break the sound barrier. He put the vehicle in gear and pulled out onto Lincoln Street. He drove several blocks and parked in front of Cokey's and Margie's house. Margie was waiting on the front porch. She looked very pretty in her long black dress and low-heeled pumps. A three-strand pearl necklace hung gracefully around her neck. Margie's short red hair was swept back from her face. She looked like a middle-aged Annette Bening.

Jake got out and walked to the porch. "Hey, Aunt Margie. Shouldn't you grab a coat? It's freezing."

"No, I'm fine," she answered.

Jake opened the back passenger door for her. Getting in, Margie said to Katherine, "I had to unpack this dress from mothballs."

"No way. I would have smelled it," Katherine joked.

"Okay, cat's out of the bag. I found this dress online and I fell in love with it." Margie beamed.

"You look gorgeous," Jake said, getting in.

"Do you like my pearls? They're a wedding present from your uncle Cokey," Margie said, with a wide smile on her face.

The trio arrived at the gala event. Two young men dressed in tuxedos greeted the guests. One of them Katherine recognized. Ken Smith, her student from the last training class, said, "Lookin' good, Teach!" Katherine smiled and said thank you.

Erie's proud mayor, Ralph Newman, rushed over and personally applauded Margie for her outstanding work. "You did an excellent job," he said, pumping her hand.

"Thank you, Mayor," Margie said. "Allow me to introduce you to my friend, Katherine Kendall."

"Hello, Katherine. Nice to see you again. It's nice to see you, Jake, as well. How's the university treating you?"

"Just fine, Mayor," Jake answered, smiling.

"Well, folks, there's a lonely bartender over there. Open bar. Help yourself." The mayor left the group and flitted off to greet the next arrivals.

Margie said, "This building was the town's library from the 1870s until the 1920s. It was slated for demolition, but I stepped in and convinced the town to give it to me."

Katherine asked, surprised, "Seriously, the town gave it to you?"

"I paid a dollar for it. State law allowed it. After I had re-roofed, updated the plumbing and electrical, and painted it, Mark Dunn approached me about making it into a museum. That was after Carol Lombard passed away and the money for the new building disappeared."

Katherine remembered, "Carol had two hundred thousand from my great aunt's will to help build a new museum, but Margie, she died before the distribution. The money is probably still available. Contact Mark Dunn about it."

"Oh, I know," Margie said. "The Erie Historical Society savings were stolen by Frank and Beatrice, but the money for the new museum came from your great aunt's will. The renovation didn't cost two hundred grand. There was money left over for miscellaneous stuff, like the displays and exhibits, heating and cooling, but not enough to pay employees. That's why the Society has volunteers to maintain it."

"Interesting," Katherine said. "Just curious. Who's the treasurer?"

"Robbie Brentwood," Margie answered, then changing the subject said, "See the display cases? I found them at a salvage store in Indy. They're original from the 1920s. The wood is oak."

The small building was wall-to-wall with display cases of various widths and heights placed against the wall. Large print placards or photo posters were mounted above. Margie continued, "The floor was in terrible shape, so I put down a laminate that looks like hardwood. It will be easier to maintain and handle foot traffic."

"Margie, you did an incredible job," Mark Dunn congratulated as he approached. On his arm was a stunning blond, long-haired with big blue-violet eyes. She was dressed in a low-cut red dress. Katherine recognized her immediately. It was Linda Martin, the Indiana state police detective who helped solve the William Colfax bootlegging mystery. Katherine had only seen her in uniform or in casual clothes. Normally, she wore her hair tied back with little cosmetics. But tonight she looked like a runway model.

"Hello. You've met Linda," Mark said cheerfully.

"Yes, of course." Katherine pulled Linda aside and said, "You look spectacular!"

Linda whispered, "Mark called me last night and asked me to join him, and I said 'yes.' I borrowed this dress from my roommate. Fortunately, we're the same size."

"Lucky you. It's perfect." Then to Mark, "Have you started working at the new firm?"

"I start on Monday. My office here is officially closed. I think Robbie Brentwood is going to rent it."

"I'm very happy for you."

"Katz, you know how to find me if you need me. Just call, text or whatever."

After Mark and Linda moved away, Jake took Katherine's arm. He led her to the first display case which housed items from the 1840s, when the town of Erie was founded. Above the glass case was a framed poster describing the importance of the Erie canal and the town's early economy. The next display case was full of photos from the tornado of 1909, which wiped out several downtown businesses. But the most popular display, and where the most people were gathered, was the William Colfax exhibit. Since there was so much material, Margie had used a separate, smaller room for that exhibit. Margie was standing near the entryway.

Katherine stopped in her tracks. There, right in front of her, was the speakeasy door from the yellow brick house. Margie caught her eye and winked.

"Margie, I can't believe how you restored this. It looks brand new."

"Trust me. It took lots of varnish remover and a light sanding, but isn't she a beauty?" Margie took Katherine by the arm and led her inside the William Colfax exhibit. The small room was lined with more display cases, blown-up posters of both William's and Orvenia's portraits, and a large framed picture of the pink mansion circa 1911.

"Emily Bradworth did a wonderful job," Katherine said. She then told Margie about how Lilac almost thwarted the young graphic artist's efforts to photograph the portraits.

Margie whispered, "She hangs out here a lot. I don't know what she sees in that Robbie guy."

Katherine shrugged. "Love is blind!"

Several mannequins in the corner wore vintage dresses from Orvenia's collection: one figure wore a beaded flapper dress from the 1920s, and the other sported a 1950s party dress, complete with a full skirt.

For security reasons, none of the gold coins found at the Ethel cemetery were exhibited, because they had been sold to a wealthy coin collector. Several of the bootlegging bottles were included, along with William's ledger and the money bag from the Greencastle Dillinger bank robbery. Katherine had the final word in where it should go, and chose to keep it in Erie.

More guests filtered into the room, so Margie and Katherine went back outside. A woman in a short, silver-sequined cocktail dress came over and introduced herself as the high school principal, Julie Miller. She asked Margie, "Where's Robbie? He's the curator, for heaven's sake. What happened to him?"

"I have no idea," Margie answered. "After the fundraiser, I came over here for a few minutes to drop off something. He was here with Emily and you."

Julie's face clouded immediately. "I don't know what you're talking about. I haven't seen Robbie since yesterday," she said, with anger rising in her voice.

"I beg to differ," Margie said defensively. "It was either you or your clone."

"If you see him, send him my way." Julie walked away with a tight-lipped expression.

Margie whispered in Katz's ear. "Want to hear some Erie gossip?"

Katherine smiled. "Sure. Why not?"

"Julie's having an affair with Robbie. It's all over town. Her husband found out and threatened to kill Robbie if he didn't leave his wife alone."

"What?" Katherine asked, puzzled.

"You want me to repeat it, kiddo?" Margie offered.

"Emily Bradworth told me the two of them were getting married, and that Robbie was going to announce it tonight."

"That's a good one," Margie said, surprised.

"If he's seeing Julie, he really is a jerk."

"Why?"

"Because that poor naïve girl moved to Erie to be with him."

"Naïve?" Margie laughed. "You mean crazy. What person in their right mind would want to move to Erie? Oops, I didn't mean you, Katz."

"What are you two whispering about?" Jake said, moving over.

"That men are good," Katherine smiled.

"You lie," he said. Then he whispered in her ear, "But you're a gorgeous liar."

She punched him affectionately on the arm.

As the evening wore on, the financial advisor/volunteer curator/cake auctioneer and apparent philanderer was an obvious "no show."

Later, Russell Krow caught Katherine coming out of the ladies room and said, "We meet again."

"Hello," she said to the handsome reporter. "Did you just get here? I didn't see you earlier." Katherine hoped he wouldn't interpret her last comment as an expression of interest.

"I'm just here to take a few pics for the paper. Then I have a deadline to meet."

"Reporter *and* photographer," she commented. "Cool."

"I'm late because I'm also a wedding photographer. I just got back from the city. You wouldn't know of anyone who is getting married and wants a photographer?"

"Can't think of anyone," Katherine answered, inching away and discretely looking for Jake to rescue her, but he was busy talking to the doctor and her husband.

"I'm new to the Erie beat and I don't know very many people. I hear you just moved from New York City. I do hope we can meet for lunch soon."

"Of course," she said with one foot poised to make her escape.

Russell continued, "I just started an Erie Community web page. Pictures that don't make the newspaper will be posted on the website. I took some wonderful pics at the fundraiser today. You've got to check them out."

"I will."

The mayor made a dash over and tapped Russell on the shoulder. "I've been meaning to talk to you about . . . "

Katherine made her exit to find Jake, who was now looking for her.

"There you are," he said, holding a plate. "They just brought out these appetizers. Do you want to try one?" He had an ornery grin on his face.

Katherine glanced at his plate loaded with puffy cheese bites. "Let me guess. Baked by Vicky the caterer and they explode at will. I'll pass." She remembered her Halloween party and how the appetizers seemed to have it out for her.

The museum event was a big success. Margie received lots of compliments. Guests asked

Katherine countless questions about the Colfax exhibit. In between glasses of champagne, Katherine's head began to spin. She grew tired of answering the same questions about her bootlegging great uncle, and was thankful when Jake came to her rescue. He was a godsend. In his true history-professor fashion, he explained Prohibition and how important bootlegging was to the Erie economy. He was in his element and enjoying it immensely. The evening was a happy occasion — a fun mix of people, holiday cheer, an open bar, and savory appetizers.

A few minutes after eleven, Julie Miller — screaming at the top of her lungs — ran from the back of the museum to the main room. "Help! Someone's murdered Robbie. He's dead!"

Mayor Newman said firmly, "Julie, calm down. Where's Robbie?"

Julie sobbed, "In the utility closet by the kitchen. He did it!" She shook an accusing finger toward the rear.

"Who did it?" the mayor asked as he headed to the back of the museum.

"Cokey Cokenberger! He killed Robbie." The distraught woman collapsed to the floor and cried, "My Robbie . . . no, not my Robbie."

Her husband Nick came to her side. "Get up! You're causing a scene."

All eyes turned from Julie to Margie. "That's a lie," Margie said. "Cokey's home with our kids."

"You don't call my wife a liar," Nick threatened.

"Okay, Nick, relax," Jake barked, rushing over to stand between the irate Nick and his aunt Margie.

Detective Linda Martin called after the

mayor. "Don't touch anything. I'm getting Chief

London over here ASAP." She yanked her cell out

of her evening bag and joined the mayor outside the

utility room. Katherine, Jake and Margie followed

her. The mayor moved to the front of the hallway

and with the help of Mark, formed a barrier so none

of the other guests could approach the area.

Jake and Margie walked into the kitchen.

Through the utility room door, and looking over

Detective Martin's shoulder, Katherine could see a

very dead Robbie. He had been stabbed repeatedly.

Strangely, there was blood on his white shirt, but

only a few splatters on the floor. They could see a

partial shoeprint on one of the blood spots. A knife

lay nearby. Someone had crudely stuffed dollar bills

in his mouth. The inside of Robbie's shirt was

stuffed with them as well. A colorful Hawaiian

necktie was knotted tightly around his neck. It

wasn't clear what had killed him — the stab wounds, or strangulation.

Detective Martin visually examined Robbie through the doorway and confirmed he was dead. "Folks, this is now a crime scene."

The mayor announced to the group. "We're sorry for Robbie's loss, but please everyone stay put until the chief gets here."

"Why can't we leave?" Nick said defiantly.

Katherine rushed to the kitchen.

Margie whispered urgently to Jake and Katherine, "We need to go — now!"

Jake directed them to the back entrance off the kitchen. As they rushed out of the museum, they could hear Detective Martin address the guests, "No one leaves until the police have interviewed you."

Chapter Six

As she left the museum building, Katherine tried to run in her Gucci pumps but slid on a patch of ice and fell into a snowdrift. Margie was already at the car and didn't see the accident. She yelled, "Jake, hurry up, you've got to get me home as soon as possible."

Jake rushed to Katherine's side. "Are you okay?" he asked, helping her up. "Do you think you broke anything?"

"Only my vanity," Katherine said, embarrassed. "I can't run in my new shoes."

Jake picked her up and threw her over his shoulder. "I'll carry you, baby doll."

Shivering, she said, "I left my coat."

"I'll get it tomorrow," Jake answered, setting her down. "Here, wear my suit jacket." He hurriedly took it off and draped it over Katherine's shoulders.

Once they were in the car, Jake floored the accelerator and took Margie home. Parking in front of the house, he had barely stopped the car when Margie jumped out and ran up the front walk. Ten-year-old Shelly was standing on the porch in her pajamas, and was crying her head off.

Jake and Katherine got out and met each other on the sidewalk.

"Daddy's hurt," Shelly cried. "He's bleeding."

"Shelly, sweetie, what happened?" Margie asked.

The girl sobbed some more. "He went to get pizza and when he got home he was bleeding. Mommy, you've got to help him."

Jake looked at Katherine with concern.

Margie rushed into the house, "Cokey?"

Tommy was nearby holding a large, plump orange cat. "Dad's locked up in the bathroom. He won't open the door."

"What the hell," Margie muttered under her breath. Shelly continued sobbing. "Shelly, it's okay. Mommy's home. I'll go check on Daddy."

Jake hurried down the hall, saying, "Listen, I'll try and coax him out."

"I don't know why he's acting like this," Margie said, stunned. She raced past Jake and pounded on the bathroom door, "Cokey, let me in."

Cokey slowly opened the door with a fresh bandage on his hand.

"What's going on?" Margie demanded.

"I was in the wrong place at the wrong time."

"What do you mean?"

"I went to the museum —"

"Why?"

"You left your cell phone on the dresser so I told the kids I'd drop it off after I picked up the pizza. I didn't want anyone to see me in my ratty jacket and jeans when everyone was dressed up, so I used the museum's back door."

"What time was this?" Margie asked.

"Around eleven."

"Why did you have the kids up so late, and then leave them to go get a pizza? It makes no sense."

"We were watching a DVD and the kids got hungry. When I first got to the museum, this woman nearly knocked me down running out the door — "

"What woman?"

"Will you let me finish? What's her name? Emily something. Then the principal's husband — I think his name is Nick — came out of the utility

174

room. I asked him to give you your cell phone. He looked like he'd just seen a ghost, and was really nervous. He took the phone and walked to the front of the museum. I got suspicious and went inside the room and found Robbie slumped on a stool."

"What was the principal's husband doing in that room?" Margie asked.

"Beats the hell out of me," Cokey said, throwing up his hands. "But when I tried to help Robbie, a butcher knife fell out of his neck. The blade must have grazed my hand because I started bleeding. When I reached in my pocket for my phone to call 911, Julie Miller ran in and started accusing me of murdering Robbie. I panicked and got the hell out of there. Now the damn knife has my prints on it, and I'm going to be framed for killing Robbie."

"But you didn't do it," Margie implored. "You've got to tell the chief that. Why didn't you just explain to Julie what happened?"

"She was hysterical and wouldn't stop screaming. Margaret, I have that misdemeanor conviction on my record. I don't want to go to prison," Cokey said.

Katherine gave Jake a curious side glance. Jake shook his head and mouthed the words, "I'll tell you later."

They heard the sound of police sirens coming down Alexander Street. Two Erie cruisers pulled in front.

Tommy, still holding the orange cat, was standing by the window and shouted, "Dad, there's a whole bunch of cops out there."

"I'll get the door," Cokey said, coming down the hall with Margie by his side. "It's okay, son. Get your sister and take her and Spitfire to your room."

Tommy ignored the request and opened the door. Chief London walked in. He was flanked by several officers.

Shelly began wailing again. "Daddy's hurt," she cried. Katherine moved over and put her arm around her. She led Shelly down the hall, then motioned for Tommy to come, too. Spitfire struggled to get down, but Tommy held him tight.

Chief London cuffed Cokey and then read him the Miranda warning.

Margie said, horrified, "Chief, what's this about?"

The chief answered, "We're arresting Cokey for the murder of Robbie Brentwood. We have an eye witness who saw Cokey leaving the scene of the crime with blood dripping from his hand."

Margie protested, "He didn't do it!"

Katherine returned to the room and gasped, "Chief, he didn't do it. Cokey just explained what happened." Then she remembered overhearing Cokey threaten Robbie at the mansion during the tea.

The officers took Cokey by the arms and led him outside. Cokey called back to Margie, "Get me a good criminal lawyer. I love you."

Chief London stayed behind. "I want to talk to the three of you. According to Detective Martin, you left the scene when Robbie's body was found. What was the hurry?"

Margie sat down on a chair and began to cry. She then calmed herself and said, "Chief, everyone in this town could be a suspect."

"How's that?" the chief asked.

"Because everyone had a beef with Robbie Brentwood. For starters, I'll give you some suspects. How about Nick Miller? He threatened to kill Robbie if he didn't leave his wife alone. How about the girlfriend, Emily? I heard her fighting with Robbie at the museum a few hours before the opening. Want me to keep goin'?" Margie said angrily.

"Be my guest," the chief said, irritated.

"What about me?" Margie continued.

Jake intervened, "Aunt Margie, the chief is just trying to get the facts."

The chief said, "You may be the last person to see Robbie alive. Why were you at the museum?"

"I'm a volunteer. After the holiday fundraiser at the armory, I stopped by to drop off some flyers for the door greeters to pass out when the guests arrived. Emily was shouting at Robbie —"

"Who's Emily?"

"She's the museum's graphic artist. She was hanging posters on the wall. When she heard Robbie's voice in the back room —"

"The utility room?"

"No, the kitchen. When she went back there, they started yelling at each other. They got into a big argument."

"What were they arguing about?"

"I don't know. I could hear their tone but not their words. When I looked out the window, Julie Miller was running to her car. Chief, Julie was having an affair with Robbie."

Katherine, who had been quiet, added, "Chief, maybe Emily caught Robbie and Julie in a compromising position and freaked out. She told me a few days ago when she came over to my house that Robbie was going to announce their engagement at the opening. Maybe she should be a person of interest." She remembered the fang-marked card from Emily, but didn't want to mention the cats' involvement, if there was an involvement. Just a clue, perhaps. A big one.

The chief said to Margie, "Anything else you want to tell me?"

Margie shook her head. "My husband didn't do it. He's the fall guy because everyone knows Cokey has a temper, and that Patricia Marston business."

The chief scratched his beard, "What about you, Jake? Why did you flee the scene?"

Jake shrugged his shoulders and said nonchalantly, "Because the ladies wanted to go home and I'm the driver."

"Okay, that's all I need to hear . . . for right now. I'm sure Detective Martin will want to talk to you, but not tonight. We've got our hands full with this mess."

As the chief moved to the door, Margie got up and asked, "Where will Cokey be?"

"Holding cell down at the jail. Don't fret, Ma'am. We'll get to the bottom of this." He tipped his hat and left.

When the chief was out of earshot, Jake said, "Aunt Margie, I'm calling Dad. Let's get him over here to talk about what we should do."

Margie choked back a sob and said, "I need the kids to go to their grandparents' house."

"I'll call them," Jake said, leaving the room. He walked outside and stood on the porch to use his cell. Katherine stayed with Margie and tried to console her. When Jake returned, he said, "Okay, Dad's on his way. Mom's coming over to take the kids to Grandpa Cokenberger's."

Margie nodded thanks and then said to Katherine, "Katz, go home, kiddo. I'll call you in the morning."

"But Margie, are you sure you don't want me to stay?" Katherine asked, genuinely concerned.

"No," Margie said, shaking her head. Tears had reformed in her eyes. "I'll be okay."

Jake said to Katherine, "I'll take you home."

"Okay, Margie, but if you need me for anything, just call."

Jake escorted Katherine out of the house and back into the car. On the way to the pink mansion, he reached over and held her hand. "Cokey's been in trouble with the law before."

"What was that about a misdemeanor?"

"It's been a million years ago. I guess these kind of things come back to haunt you."

"What kind of things?" Katherine asked adamantly, wanting him to just tell her.

"When he was dating Patricia Marston, the two of them were involved in a minor car wreck. Patricia was acting weird, so the officer searched the car and found marijuana. Cokey didn't want her to get arrested, because she had a former conviction. So he took the fall for her. He pled guilty and got probation and some sort of conditional release, with no jail time. But I guess there's still a permanent record. That's when he broke off the engagement to Patricia."

"It's all starting to gel," Katherine said, then added, "But, why would Cokey have an affair with Patricia with this thing hanging over his head?"

Jake just shook his head. He climbed out of the car and walked over to the passenger side. Katherine had already opened the door and was getting out. She said, "Call or text me as soon as you learn anything."

Jake held her in a quick embrace. "Sure thing, sweet pea."

They quietly walked to the front of the house. Scout and Abra were sitting inside the parlor window, watching the couple curiously. Katherine turned the key in the lock and said, "I'll see you tomorrow."

Jake nodded and turned to leave. Katherine went inside to find three cats waiting for her. Scout and Abra didn't waste time joining them. Taking Jake's suit jacket off, which she'd forgotten to return, she hung it on the Eastlake hall tree. She sat down on the floor and asked, "How about a group hug?" The cats looked at her inquisitively, but didn't move in for the 'hug.' She knew they had special 'sleuth' abilities, but wasn't quite sure how and why they did the things they did. "My treasures, I'm leaving my computer on. Google me a clue as to who killed Robbie Brentwood." She said it out of jest more than anything else.

Scout gave her a long, hard look and then trotted to the office. "Waugh," she cried. The other cats took off and followed her.

Katherine got up with an amazed look on her face. *That was strange*, she thought. *I think I'll faint if I go to my office and find one of them surfing the web.*

She kicked off her Gucci pumps and walked in her bare feet to the office, a little bit afraid of what she'd see, but instead found the cats in the kitchen, hovering over their empty food bowls.

"Fakers! You just want a bedtime snack."

"Ma-waugh," Scout agreed.

She removed the kibble jar and scooped out food for each cat. Turning out the kitchen light, she said, "Bon appétit!"

*　　*　　*

The next morning, Colleen and Katherine were sitting at the kitchen table when Mrs. Murphy walked in.

"Top of the mornin'," she said in her heavy Irish brogue, then laughed.

Katherine got up. "Sit here. I'll get you some tea or coffee. I just made a pot of hazelnut."

Mrs. Murphy sat down. "Never had hazelnut. I'd love a cup. I hope you slept well," she said to Katherine, completely oblivious to what had transpired the night before.

The morning *Erie Herald* lay flat on the table, its front page covered with photos of the fundraiser, museum event, and a large picture of the late financial advisor/curator/cake auctioneer.

"What's happenin' in the paper?" Mrs. Murphy asked, picking it up. An expression of shock came over her face. "Robbie Brentwood is dead? Murdered? His mother must be beside herself with grief."

"It was a grave ending to an otherwise gala museum opening. The police are still trying to piece together what happened," Katherine said, pouring the coffee and handing her the cup.

Colleen passed the cream and sugar. Mrs. Murphy reached in her robe pocket for her flask, but then put it away. Colleen looked relieved.

Katherine proceeded to fill Mum in on the events at the museum, including Cokey's arrest. She'd already discussed the situation with Colleen.

Colleen said, "Katz, you need to write a book. This place is like an American horror story. Something sinister is always happening."

"And usually it involves you, Miss Katz," Mrs. Murphy said candidly. "I worry about you livin' here alone."

"At least this time, the murder wasn't at the mansion."

Colleen glanced at the paper. "I love the photo Mr. Hunk took of Jake holding Lilac. That is *so precious*. But what's this?" Colleen hesitated. "Anonymous donor gives one hundred thousand dollars to the Erie Food Bank." Colleen looked up from the paper at Katherine, who was smiling.

"It was the price I had to pay for Lilac's demolition," she chuckled. "Actually, I made the donation a few days ago. I kind of like the idea of being anonymous for future donations, as well."

Colleen fidgeted with her spoon. "Katz, Mum and I have something to tell you."

"What?" Katherine asked with concern. "Judging by your change in facial expression, should I expect doom-and-gloom?"

"No," Colleen said with a serious look. "You start, Mum."

Mrs. Murphy put two sugar cubes in her coffee. "Katz, I've been thinkin' a lot about this business with my building goin' condo. I don't want to buy my apartment, so I'm goin' to have to move —"

Katherine said happily. "Yay! Are you moving here?"

There was an uncomfortable pause, and then Mrs. Murphy shook her head. "No, I'm not movin' to Indiana, but if it's okay with you, I want to move into your apartment in Manhattan and live with my son, Jacky."

"That's okay, but there's only two bedrooms. Where are you going to sleep?"

Colleen broke in, "Remember at your Halloween party how that Russian fortune teller said I'd make a long-distance move? I thought she meant I was moving to Italy to join Mario, but in reality, she predicted I was moving to Indiana to be with Daryl. Katz, I'm moving out here."

"What?" Katherine asked, surprised. She clapped her hands. "Should I jump up and down?"

Lilac and Abby flew into the kitchen and hopped on the counter. "I didn't mean to call you guys," she explained to the cats, who looked like they'd just gotten up from a nap. "This is great news. You can live here with me."

"You know I'd love to, but I'm going to rent an apartment in the city and go to school. I've hated my job forever. My boss is a jerk. I want to become a teacher."

"I think you'd make a *great* teacher," Katherine complimented.

"So, Katz, I'm going to fly back, quit my job, and move out here in January. Daryl is going to help me find an apartment close to campus."

Mrs. Murphy gave a conspiratorial smile from across the table. "Guess who's helpin' her move?"

Katherine knew Mum referred to Daryl, but said, "You want me to rent an old beat-up Toyota and come and get you?"

"Oh, yes, by all means. And bring the cats in one carrier," Colleen joked. "Actually, Daryl is helping me."

192

"Daryl, huh? I forgot to ask. How did dinner go?" She didn't give Colleen time to answer. She hurriedly asked Mum, "What did you think of Daryl and his parents?"

"'Twas a grand meetin'. Daryl was the perfect gentleman, and I like the way he treats my daughter."

Colleen added, "His parents are sweet. I was a nervous wreck, but they made me feel at home immediately."

"Cool! It's a Cokenberger thing," Katherine smiled. "Well, not so much Cokey, but Jake's a keeper, too."

The kitchen phone rang noisily.

Katherine moved to the phone and answered it. "Hello?"

"Hey, kiddo, it's Margie. Good news. Cokey was released an hour ago," she began.

"Oh, that's wonderful. So the charges have been dropped?"

"Yes and no. It's complicated. Can I come over? There have been some curious twists in Robbie's case," she continued.

"Sure, come to the side door. We're eating breakfast. What do you take in your coffee?"

"Black and straight up," Margie said.

Within five minutes, Margie pulled in the driveway and parked Cokey's Dodge Ram behind Katherine's Subaru. Katherine met her at the door.

"This is such good news," Katherine said. "Come in and tell us what happened."

Margie broke into an uneasy smile and walked in the kitchen. She said hello to Mrs. Murphy and Colleen. She took off her navy-blue pea jacket, threw it over the aluminum chair, and sat down.

Katherine passed a steaming coffee cup her way. Margie began, "Detective Martin just left my house." She took a sip and said, "Cokey is still a person of interest, but there isn't enough evidence, based on the coroner's estimated time of death, to charge him with murdering Robbie Brentwood."

"That's kind of in limbo until they find out who did it," Katherine suggested.

"Detective Martin said they were working on the assumption that Robbie died of strangulation because of the lack of blood at the crime scene."

Mrs. Murphy turned a lighter shade of pale. "I'm off to me room to get dressed." She got up abruptly and left the room.

Margie's face reddened. "I'm so sorry. I should have told her I was going to be talking about gory stuff."

"No worries," Katherine assured.

Colleen leaned in and asked, "So, if the poor man was strangled, why would somebody stab him?"

Margie shook her head, "They don't know, but I'm just happy Cokey is home with me and the kids. I can't wait for this to be over." She got up. "I've got to get back home. Thanks for the coffee. I can show myself out." She put on her pea jacket and left. Katherine followed her to make sure the door was locked.

Returning to the kitchen, Katherine said, "That was awkward."

"What part?" Colleen asked. "The fact that Cokey is a person of interest? Or Margie's undying conviction that her husband is a knight in shining armor?"

"I've wondered that myself. Most of the time I think Cokey is a good guy with some personal problems, but lately I'm thinking he's not what he appears to be. Could he have killed Robbie?"

Colleen answered, "For the love of Mary, I hope not."

"I hope not either."

Chapter Seven

The following Friday evening, Katherine, Colleen, and Linda Martin met for drinks at the pink mansion. The Indiana State Police investigator was off-duty. The three of them sat around the glass-topped Parsons table, munching on tortilla chips with salsa and guacamole dip. Linda sprang out of her chair and asked, "Who wants another margarita?"

Scout, Abra and Iris were stretched out on the floor register, basking in the artificial heat. Scout opened one eye at the detective's enthusiasm, emitted a "waugh," then covered it with her paw and went back to sleep.

"Hit me with your best shot," Colleen joked, holding up her glass.

"I'm good," Katherine answered. "They're really good. I want the recipe."

Linda winked, "It's very scientific."

"Do I need a chemistry degree to understand it?" Katherine mused.

"Using a standard shot glass: one and a half shots of tequila, one shot of orange liqueur — I use Cointreau — and two shots of lime juice. Serve over crushed ice with the glass rimmed with salt. Okay, gals, this is the last one. My margaritas are *very* strong."

After Linda made the drinks and sat back down, Katherine proposed a toast. "I'd like to toast the state of Indiana for granting Detective Martin a night off so she could come over and make these awesome margaritas."

"Hear, hear!" Colleen seconded.

The three clinked their glasses.

Colleen said to Linda impishly, "What have you been doing lately?"

Linda's grin flashed and quickly disappeared. "Robbie Brentwood's murder case is the most baffling one I've ever investigated," she began. "I can't talk about it in minute detail, but I can say what the media is privy to. Poor Robbie was strangled with his own necktie and then stabbed. But," Linda paused, then said, "This is the fascinating part. He died from some kind of fast-acting poison. The toxicology lab in Indy is trying to identify exactly what kind of chemical it was."

"Let me get this straight," Katherine said. "He died from the poisoning first, then was strangled and stabbed? Sounds like the Rasputin case." Katherine referred to the Russian mystic, who was a private advisor to the Romanovs and a player in the downfall of the Russian monarchy. Rasputin was assassinated in 1916.

"Close, but Rasputin wasn't strangled. He was shot multiple times."

Colleen interjected, "Geez, you two, how do you know this stuff?"

"History Channel," Katherine admitted.

Linda continued, "It was exhausting interviewing all those people at the museum opening. They were cranky and just wanted to go home. It was three o'clock in the morning before I hit the sack."

Katherine added, "I'm sorry that Margie, Jake and I didn't stay to be interviewed, but we'd already cleared the back door when I heard you order everyone to remain. Margie was desperate to get home."

"Understandably, considering Julie Miller's accusation of Cokey murdering Robbie," Linda agreed.

Katherine asked, "Just curious, but did Mark stay the whole time? I guess you never thought in a million years a murder would interfere with your first date."

"I couldn't see any reason for Mark to stick around, so I asked him to go home. Chief London took me home later."

Colleen leaned forward and asked curiously. "So, what do you think of Mark?"

Linda smiled. "Can you two keep a secret?"

"Of course," Katherine said. "Who are we going to tell? It's not like we know anyone in town."

"He asked me out for a second date. Tomorrow night we're going to Indy to this restaurant he's gaga over. I hope the weather doesn't ruin our plans."

Katherine scrunched her face, "More snow tomorrow. Sorry, didn't mean to jinx it."

Colleen suggested, "If the weather's bad, why don't Mark and you just go to one of the local restaurants?"

"Mark doesn't want the town's gossips to be talking about us. He's very private in his personal life —"

"I can vouch for that," Katherine said. "I've known him since last February, and I still don't *know* him."

"He's a really good guy," Linda said. "Funny, smart and likes the same kind of things I do. I'm just thankful for the second date," she sighed.

"What do you mean?" Katherine asked.

"Because when men find out I'm an investigator for the state police, they run. Did I mention they *run*?"

As if on cue, Lilac and Abby ran into the room, jumped to the counter, and launched themselves over to the window valance. Abby had a caged ball with a bell in it clamped in her jaws.

"Whoa," Linda said, surprised. "I didn't see that coming."

Colleen laughed. "You know, Katz, since I've been here I've stepped on two of those things."

Katherine giggled, "I know. They're not long for the world. I buy them by the dozen."

Abby muffled a chirp, turned her head and threw the ball. It bounced on the table and landed in the guacamole dip.

"Abigail," Katherine scolded. Abby stretched up into a tall, noble pose.

Colleen and Linda burst out laughing.

In an acrobatic feat worthy of a trapeze artist, Abby effortlessly soared over Lilac to the other side of the valance, to the counter, and then to the floor. She trotted out of the room.

"I'll get some more dip." Katherine moved to the refrigerator, opened the door, and removed a package. Stepping back to the table she confessed, "It's store-bought, but you've gotta admit, it's quite tasty."

Abby trotted back into the room, leaped up onto the table, and dropped a poly-wrapped syringe in front of Linda.

Linda startled. "What the hell? What is that?"

Abby scampered out of the room in search of another toy to show the humans.

Katherine nervously drummed her fingers on the table, "I think I might know who it belongs to."

Colleen added doubtfully, "Well, since Mum and I aren't diabetic, it definitely doesn't belong to us."

Linda asked, "Okay, Katz, who and what?"

Katherine inhaled slowly. "I don't know where to start. Emily Bradworth came over to the mansion to photograph my great aunt's and uncle's portraits. She's a graphic artist and was going to make posters for the museum, which she did. One of my cats started bugging her, so she came back to my office to get me. When we returned to the living room, the cats had dumped her camera case. Emily became upset — well, I mean troubled — because when she put everything back in the case, she said there was something missing. She was down on her hands and knees, searching, but she wouldn't tell me for what. She finally gave up and said she'd probably left it at home. I told her I'd call if I found anything, but she didn't give me her phone number."

"Do you think she was looking for this syringe?" Linda asked.

"My cats are thieves. Before she left, I looked in the place where they usually hide their loot —"

"Loot? Your cats actually steal things and hide them? Smart cats," Linda said, amused.

"The cats must have hidden it somewhere else. I mean, Abby hid it and just brought it in here to play with."

Colleen disagreed. "Katz, Robbie and his mother were here. Maybe Lizard is diabetic." Colleen clearly was convinced the syringe was for insulin.

Linda picked up the hypodermic needle and read the print on the plastic package. "Heartland Aquarium, Chicago."

Katherine said hurriedly, "I have a hunch that Emily's mom works there. She said her mom was a marine biologist in Chicago. Did you talk to Emily?"

Linda was slightly taken aback. "Well, no, I can't find her. I checked all our databases. She has an Illinois driver's license. But since Robbie was murdered, it's as if she simply vanished. No paper trail. No credit card use. No sightings. I'm worried she may have met the same fate as Robbie. When I asked Robbie's mother if she knew where Emily was, she was too traumatized by her son's death to talk coherently. In fact, she didn't even know who Emily was."

"But what about the address on the driver's license?" Katherine asked.

"Oh, that was a dead-end. The address was an apartment building that was recently demolished for a parking garage. It's frustrating. Not one person I interviewed has a clue where Emily lives. Katz, you wouldn't happen to know, would you?"

"The only thing I know is that she works for a graphic design studio. Surely there aren't that many in the city. Maybe the studio's logo is on the museum posters," Katherine answered.

"I'll check. Thanks for the tip," Linda said, then volunteered, "We know Robbie and Emily were a couple. We know that he was also having an affair with another woman — a married woman."

Colleen said in a dramatic voice. "Hell hath no fury like a woman scorned."

"That's a pretty good motive for his murder," Linda said, then added, "What I'm about to tell you next is strictly private and confidential."

Colleen pantomimed her lips being zipped.

Katherine said, "You can trust us."

Linda continued, "We also know the Federal Trade Commission and the FBI were ready to make an arrest."

Katherine said, surprised. "The FBI? Why?"

"Our new financial advisor in town was running a pyramid scheme."

"Fascinating," Katherine said, and remembered nearly breaking an ankle tripping over a heavy book on the Egyptian pyramids. One of Iris's pastimes is pulling books off the bookcase shelves. Then she remembered the Siamese stampede. She thought, *my smart cats knew he was a fraud. That's why they didn't let me sign any documents.*

"What's a pyramid scheme?" Colleen asked.

"Also called a Ponzi scheme," Linda said. "In a nutshell, a Ponzi scheme is a fraudulent investing scam promising high rates of return with little risk to investors. Usually these schemes collapse when the pool of new investors dries up. Money from new investors is distributed to investors who bought in first, to sustain the illusion of real profits."

"This is terrible! I wonder how many people in Erie will lose their money?" Katherine asked, thinking of Mark and Cokey, but not mentioning their names.

Colleen dipped a chip in the salsa and said, "Maybe someone lost big-time and murdered Robbie."

Katherine agreed. "Linda, you have to remember, I saw the crime scene. Someone strangled Robbie and then stuffed dollar bills in his mouth. It seems to me to be symbolic of something — perhaps greed. I think Colleen has a point."

Linda offered, "We have a suspect in custody for Robbie's strangulation. His prints are on Robbie's necktie. But he didn't *kill* him because Robbie was already dead based on the coroner's preliminary findings."

Katherine and Colleen exchanged confused looks.

"The plot thickens," Colleen said.

Linda changed the subject. "Katz, let's get back to Emily. Why are you interested in her?"

Katherine took a sip of her margarita. "Well, because Cokey said when he went to the museum to return Margie's cell phone, Emily nearly knocked him down running out of the place. He said she looked very upset."

"I know. That's what he told me. He also said Nick Miller was at the crime scene, as well. This is public knowledge. But you didn't answer the question," Linda pursued. "Why are you interested in Emily?"

Katherine gave an angry look. "Figuratively speaking, if I were Emily, I'd want to strangle the jerk, as well —"

Colleen finished, "With the Hawaiian necktie the poor girl probably gave him when they met in Hawaii." She crossed herself and said, "The saints preserve us. It's wrong to talk about the newly departed."

Katherine continued, "He conned her into moving to Indiana, then he takes up with a married woman. Who does that? Emily was nuts about him."

"Nuts, perhaps, but not in the way you mentioned," Linda posed. She reached for her bag, which was hanging on the aluminum side chair. She unzipped it, then removed her cell phone. She began panning through pictures. "I need to check something. Colleen, when you mentioned stepping on the cat toys, it made me think of something odd at the crime scene. We found a small plastic cap, sort of like a pen cap, on the floor, but didn't know what it was. Let me enlarge this. Yes, yes," she said excitedly. "There it is." She showed the picture to Katherine and Colleen.

"It looks exactly like the cap on the syringe Abby brought in," Katherine said knowingly. She had suspected Emily all along. She remembered Scout's half-hearted Halloween dance in front of the young graphic artist.

Linda got up and swiftly put on her coat. "Excuse me, ladies. I need to make a few calls. I need to find Emily Bradworth."

Abby, who was now sitting demurely on the counter with her front paw on a yarn mouse, was watching the women with great interest.

Katherine said, "Wait just a second. If Emily did murder Robbie by injecting him with poison, how did she get it? It's not like she walked into the drug store and bought it."

Linda answered, "We need to find out where Emily's mom works, and as a marine biologist, if she has access to some fast-acting poison. If she does, we need to find out how Emily got it."

Colleen said, "That's easy. Emily stole it!"

Katherine asked, "But how did she know what to steal?"

Colleen tossed her head back and said, "I just watched this show on Animal Planet about these poisonous sea creatures from *Hawaii* that can kill a human in five minutes. Katz, you said Emily told you she visited Hawaii. Maybe she found out about it there, or from her mom."

"Whoa! That's a good lead. The CSI lab needs to test the cap found at the crime scene for a toxic substance. I'll make sure they know the aquarium connection. I'll talk to you guys later, but in the meantime, would you two brainstorming sleuths please keep quiet about this new theory?" Linda asked, rising to leave.

Katherine followed Linda to the door and said, "Keep me posted."

"Will do. See you later," Linda left and got in her car. Katherine went back to the kitchen.

Colleen was dipping another chip. "I may be a little buzzed from that margarita, but did we just solve a crime?"

Katherine laughed. "I'm not sure. We suspect Emily was that woman scorned. We know that Julie Miller was having an affair with Robbie. Our friend, Detective Martin, mentioned a male suspect being held at the jail. We know it's not Cokey because he's home with Margie and the kids. I'm banking the male suspect is Julie Miller's husband, Nick."

Colleen shook her head. "That wouldn't explain the dollar bills stuffed in Robbie's mouth.

Nick's motive was simple. His wife was cheating with Robbie."

Katherine thought for a moment, then said, "Maybe Julie invested lots of money with Robbie and when Nick found out, he confronted Robbie at the museum. When I first went to meet Robbie at his office, while I was heading out, I bumped into Nick. I didn't know him at the time, but met him at the museum opening. I heard him threaten to break someone's neck. I'm assuming it was Robbie's neck. Also, Cokey saw him leave the utility room where Robbie was murdered. But what I'm saying is pure conjecture. I'm not the detective. Just an interested bystander."

Colleen rubbed her forehead. "My brain's a bit fuzzy right now. Emily and Nick killed Robbie, but who stabbed him?"

"Multiple stab wounds indicate a hate crime. I learned that in my criminology class at NYU.

Maybe Emily came back to finish the job,"
Katherine said.

"Just in case the toxin didn't work."

"Yes, does this remind you of anything?"
Katherine asked sadly.

"Déjà vu! That Marston woman and how she
killed Gary. I'm sorry, Katz."

Katherine then thought about the movie
Gosford Park, and how one of the cats had surfed up
that page. "Colleen, care to join me in the living
room for a movie? I can Netflix it."

"Sure," Colleen said, getting up. "What
movie?"

"*Gosford Park.*"

"Oh, the saints preserve us," Colleen said,
shocked. "The movie was about a murder committed
by multiple people by different ways. Katz,
sometimes your cats can be a little bit too eerie!"

Katherine smiled. "I'll take that as a compliment."

Chapter Eight

On Monday after lunch, Katherine drove downtown to the Erie police headquarters, and asked the officer at the front desk if Chief London was available. The officer, a middle-aged man with a military-style haircut, was one she didn't recognize, new to the Erie force. He nodded and directed her to Chief London's office. The chief was sitting behind his desk with his feet up, drinking from a giant bottle of water. Between gulps he said, "Thanks, Bill," to the officer, and then to Katherine, "Did you come to chew me out about taking Cokey into custody?" He pointed toward a chair.

Katz sat down and folded her jacket on her lap. "Actually, I'm here to discuss business. Do you have a few minutes?"

"Sure," he said with a rising intonation, tugging at his beard. He threw the now-empty water bottle into the waste can. "Two points," he boasted.

220

"Initially the evidence did point to Cokey. I understand why you suspected him and brought him in for questioning. What I didn't count on was the number of ways Robbie Brentwood died."

"Yep, poisoned, strangled and stabbed." The chief shook his head. "Poisoned by his jilted girlfriend, strangled by a disgruntled husband, and then the grand finale — psycho girlfriend comes back and stabs him. Pure rage. Erie has become a regular Peyton Place," he spitted. "Cokey screwed up by leaving the crime scene and not calling 911."

"True, but if it's any consolation, Cokey is now the star witness. He saw both Emily and Nick leave the crime scene. By the way, Chief, is Emily behind bars?"

The chief nodded. "She's in custody, and her defense lawyer is arranging to have her mental competency evaluated." Changing the subject, the chief said, "Detective Martin told me how your cat was instrumental in solving the case. That's pretty damn extraordinary."

Not wanting the chief to know about her cats' special talents, Katherine downplayed the remark. "My cat thought the syringe was a toy."

"Which cat was it? The big Siamese that springs up and down like a Halloween cat?" The chief referred to Scout's death dance in front of the body of former housekeeper, Vivian Marston.

"No, not my Siamese, Scout. This time it was my great aunt's cat, Abigail. She's a bit of a thief and stole it out of Emily's camera case. You're not going to arrest Abby, are you?"

The chief emitted a laugh punctuated with short snorts. "No, I don't think I can. I don't have any cuffs that would fit her." He slapped his knee. "That was a good one," he added.

"Just out of curiosity, and you probably can't tell me, but did you hear from the lab about what kind of poison it was?"

"Actually, I can tell you. I just approved a press release and you'll hear it on the news. Emily Bradworth stole the poison from the lab where her mother works."

"At the Heartland Aquarium, right?"

The chief nodded. He sorted through some papers, picked one up and read, "South sea cone shell. Toxic, poisonous and deadly. Seems Emily wasn't as innocent as everyone thought. She stole the poison before she moved to Indiana."

"How do you know that?"

"Her mother told me. She didn't want to be fired from her job so she kept it quiet."

"So she knew her daughter had stolen it?"

"No, she suspected she did, but when she confronted her, Emily denied it."

"Emily must have suspected Robbie was a womanizer, yet she still moved here to be close to him," Katherine said.

"There's no accounting for taste. You've got to admit, for someone who is nuttier than a fruitcake, Emily was pretty clever."

"I feel sorry for her," Katherine said, and then came to the point, "I didn't come here to talk about Cokey or Emily. Soon I'll be inheriting the rest of my great aunt's estate. I'm asking various people to sit on the board — "

"Board?" he interrupted. "Oh, and by the way, congratulations. My ole buddy Mark told me you just got a check for five million."

"Is there anything in this town that's private?" she kidded, knowing that the chief and the estate attorney were close friends. "I guess it's not exactly secret. I'm thinking everyone in Erie knows it by now."

"What kind of board?" the chief asked again.

"I'm forming a board to help me distribute my money to various agencies, causes, and charities. I'll be the head of it, of course, but I want people whom I trust sitting on the board. I've grown to trust your judgment."

"I'd be honored," the chief said, flattered. Before he had time to say more, the landline rang. He reached over and put the call on speaker. "Yes," he answered gruffly in his usual police-chief way.

"Chief London, this is Sheriff Goodman. I just got a call from the Indy Women's Correctional Facility. My deputy, who was transporting a prisoner from our jail to Indy, never showed up. Prisoner's last name: Marston. Patricia. She managed to escape at the I-74 rest stop west of Brownsburg. Subject is at large and armed. She stole my deputy's gun and hit him on the head with it."

Katherine leaned forward in her seat with obvious alarm.

"What?" the chief barked into the speaker. "When was this?"

"Earlier this morning, sometime around nine o'clock. I just found out a few minutes ago. I wanted to let you know the suspect might be headed to her old stomping grounds."

"Okay, let's back up. What the hell happened?"

The Sheriff continued, "Deputy Jones was found by a couple from Illinois, slumped over in the driver's seat of the county vehicle. He was unconscious, but when he came to, he said it happened about an hour earlier. He's suffering from a concussion but is going to be okay. The Marston woman was seen by a trucker, still at the rest stop, jumping into a red pickup truck, driving across the median, and speeding northwest. I've notified the state police."

"Damn," the chief exploded. "How does a trained officer get disarmed by an *unarmed* woman riding in the back seat? Did the dumbass let her sit up front?"

"Deputy Jones is on administrative leave until we find out what the hell happened," Sheriff Goodman said defensively.

"Listen, thanks, Sheriff. Keep me informed and up-to-date." He pressed the off button and fired Katherine a worried glance.

Katherine was shaking her head. "My nightmare with this woman just won't stop. What should I do?"

"The state police will find her. It won't be long before she's in custody again," he assured. "But in the meantime, I want you to go home, pack a bag, and get out of town for a few days. Text me where you are. I'm not sayin' I can provide police surveillance. Probably can't because we don't have the manpower, but try to get away from Erie, as far as you can. Patricia's nuts. She might come after you."

Katherine hurriedly got up and walked to the door. "I'll be in touch."

The chief had grabbed the phone and was punching in a number. He waved Katherine on rather abruptly, but she understood he was angry about the latest turn of events, and he was concerned about her safety.

Katherine ran to her car, opened the door, and jumped in. Nervously fumbling with the clasp on her crossover bag, she extracted her cell and called Jake. "I've got an emergency," she said breathlessly. "Chief London wants me out of town."

"Why?" Jake asked in disbelief.

Katherine turned the ignition, floored the accelerator, and peeled out on Main Street. "Patricia Marston escaped. I'm heading to the pink mansion now. I don't have time to explain."

"Katz, I'm not far. I'll meet you there and help corral the cats. We'll decide later where to go."

Driving in front of the house, she was shocked to see a red pickup blocking her parking spot. *Surely that's not the stolen vehicle,* she thought. *Would Patricia be stupid enough to park in front when the police are looking for her?*

Quickly getting out of the car, she rushed up the steps to the front porch landing. She was startled when Mrs. Murphy opened the door.

"Hello, Katz. I was just headin' to the kitchen to make a bit of tea," she slurred.

"Whose truck is that?" Katherine asked uneasily.

Mum ignored the question. "I've been talkin' a bit of treason with your friend from the library. She's waitin' for you in the living room. I'll fix some tea."

Katherine took Mrs. Murphy by the arm. "Come with me," she insisted. She directed her to the stairwell.

Mum resisted. "Whatever 'tis the matter?"

Katherine said firmly, "Shhh! Lower your voice. Go to your room and lock the door. Call Colleen and tell her to not come back to the house until she hears from me."

"In the name of all the saints," Mum said, as she staggered upstairs.

Katherine sprinted past her to her back hallway bedroom. She pulled the Glock out of the gun safe and joined Mum outside her door.

"I'm *going* to call the police. Please relax," Katherine reassured and then, with rising alarm in her voice, "*Where* are the cats?"

"The last time I saw them, they were in the kitchen."

"Hurry! Get in your room."

Mum finally went in and locked the door.

Katherine yanked her cell out of her bag and called Chief London. "I think the vehicle Patricia Marston stole is parked in front of my house," she said anxiously. "It's a red pickup."

"Katz, stay in your vehicle. Do NOT go inside," the chief ordered. "I'll be there in a few minutes."

"That's a problem because I'm *already*

inside." She disconnected the call and tapped Jake's

number. It rang and rang, then went into voice mail.

"Don't come. Chief's on his way." She put the cell

in her back pocket.

Gripping the Glock with both hands, she

cautiously walked downstairs. Suspecting the

woman in the living room was armed, Katherine

swiftly searched downstairs, leaving the living room

for last. She had to get to the cats in the kitchen, and

shut that door so they wouldn't run into the living

room. Entering the kitchen, she was shocked to find

the cats weren't on the register or on the window

valance. *Oh, my God. They're in the living room*

with a murderer.

Walking into the living room, with her gun

poised to shoot, Katherine found Patricia Marston

sitting on the mauve loveseat. She had Abby by the

scruff of her neck and was pointing the stolen

deputy's gun at the terrified Abyssinian. "Come any closer and I'll kill her," the woman threatened, then added in a menacing voice. "Now put your freakin' gun down."

Slowly Katherine lowered her Glock, placed it carefully on the coffee table, and stepped back.

"Nice seeing you again, Ms. Kendall. I thought we'd have a little chat before I blow your head off. But for starters, I think I'll kill each of your cats, one-by-one."

"No-o-o," Katherine pleaded. "What is it you want from me? I can help you get out of the state. I can drive you wherever you want to go, but don't hurt my kids." From the corner of her eye, she could see a shape moving through the back office hallway and up behind Patricia's loveseat. It was Jake.

Katherine immediately tried to distract Patricia. "I've got money to give you. Just let me make this right."

Jake had almost reached the loveseat, when one of the wood floorboards creaked noisily. Patricia threw Abby to the floor, turned and saw him.

Abby righted herself and raced out of the room. Scout and Abra were in the short hallway doing the death dance — swaying back and forth. Their eyes were glowing red in the dim light.

Jake dove for the loveseat but Patricia was already standing up. She raised her gun and shot Jake.

Katherine lunged to the coffee table and picked up her Glock. She aimed and pulled the trigger. Her first shot hit Patricia in the arm. But, when Katherine realized that wasn't going to stop her, she aimed and fired a second shot.

Patricia returned a volley of shots, but the bullets hit the Belter chair and the stained glass transom instead. She staggered, dropped her gun, and fell back onto the loveseat. Katherine hurriedly kicked the gun out of reach.

Jake continued walking. His eyes were glazed and an expression of shock had spread on his handsome face. He then slumped to the floor.

Mum ran into the room, screaming. "What's happening?"

Katherine rushed to Jake's side. He was unconscious and losing blood. She took off her coat and removed her zip-up jacket. Using her jacket, she balled it up and applied pressure directly to Jake's wound, which was in his shoulder, just below his left collarbone.

Tears were streaming down her face, "Oh, no! Oh, no!" she kept saying in shock. The cats, led by Scout and Abra, came into the room and stood sentry over Jake's prostrate body. Their eyes seemed to reveal sadness and alarm. Scout began crying a mournful "waugh." The others joined in.

Mum said hysterically, "Katz, I can't get a hold of Colleen."

"Go to the next room and get on the house phone. Dial 911. Ask for an ambulance."

"Yes. Yes," Mum said as she rushed out of the room.

Katherine knelt next to Jake, continuing to apply pressure to the wound. "Oh, you can't leave me. I love you. I don't want to let you go," she cried.

Katherine could hear sirens in the distance, getting louder and closer. An ambulance pulled in front of the mansion with Chief London's cruiser behind it. Mrs. Murphy went to the front door and opened it wide. She directed the paramedics to the living room. They dashed over to Jake. Chief

London and Officer Troy ran in after them. They

quickly sized up the situation, and went to Patricia.

Katherine was on autopilot. Voices around

her were close but sounded distant and distorted.

Maybe it was because of the deafening sound of the

gun blasts. She didn't know. She heard Chief

London pronounce Patricia dead. Another voice

said, "We've gotta get him to the trauma center in

the city." She heard a second voice call it in.

Another person came in. "Chopper's goin' to land at

the high school football field. Gotta get him in the

bus and transport him there ASAP." A female

medic's voice said to Katherine, "Ma'am, please

move aside. I'll take over."

Chief London said to Officer Troy, "Make

sure no one is on the football field and secure the

area. Katz," he said, moving over to her and helping

her to her feet. "It's going to be okay. I'm calling

Jake's parents right now. I want them to swing by and pick you up to take you to the hospital."

Katherine said, "I can drive."

"No hell you ain't. I've seen you drive."

"Okay, agreed. Chief London, I didn't mean to kill her, but she kept firing."

"The way I see it, it was self-defense. We'll talk about this another time."

Katherine was in shock. This was her worst nightmare. All she could see was the man she wanted to spend the rest of her life with, bleeding on the floor of the pink mansion. *If only I'd stayed in Manhattan,* she thought. *Jake wouldn't be dying on the floor.*

The gurney was wheeled in and Jake was carefully lifted and placed on it. He moaned once but his eyes didn't open. Katherine tried to move with him, but too many people were surrounding the gurney. Jake was rolled outside, then loaded up into the bus. When the ambulance left with lights flashing and siren wailing, she collapsed on her knees on the frozen sidewalk and began sobbing. Daryl and Colleen drove up and got out of the Impala. Daryl ran over, "Is Jake alive?"

Katherine nodded.

He squeezed her shoulder and then joined the officers and medical personnel pouring in and out of the mansion, including the coroner, who had just arrived. Colleen ran for Katherine and knelt down next to her. She held her friend in her arms and rocked her. "Katz, I'm here. It's going to be okay. What happened? Katz, talk to me. What's going on?"

Katherine stammered, "She shot Jake and then I shot her. She's dead."

"For the love of Mary, who is *she*?" Colleen implored, terrified.

"Patricia Marston. I killed her. I shot her and she's dead."

Colleen comforted. "Katz, we've got to go inside and make sure Mum and the cats are all right," she said, getting up. She held her hand out to Katherine who slowly got up. They walked into the mansion and began looking for the cats.

They found Mrs. Murphy sitting on an atrium Eastlake chair, drinking from her flask.

"Not now, mother," Colleen thundered. "I need your wits about you to help us. Have you seen the cats?"

Mrs. Murphy said, "I want to go home. This wretched place is terrible. Get me out of here."

"Calm down, Mum."

"Colleen," Katherine cried from the dining room. "We've got to get the cat carriers out of the office. After we find the cats, I want you to drive mum and the kids to the bungalow. Stay there tonight. Put the cats in their room."

"Of course, Katz."

Katherine removed her car keys from her pocket and handed them to Colleen.

Daryl came into the room and said, "Katz, can you come here *quick*. We've got a problem with your cats."

Katherine hurried into the living room and found Scout and Abra doing their Halloween death dance in front of Patricia's lifeless body. "Hiss," Scout shrieked. Abra was foaming at the mouth, ejecting spittle around her as she shook her head. Scout hissed again and growled a long, menacing growl.

The coroner, police and medical personnel stood back, not knowing what to do. Katherine stooped down in front of the frenzied pair and began talking to them in a soothing voice. "It's okay. Mommy's going to take you out of here." She managed to snatch both and take them into her office. Colleen was right behind and grabbed the carriers out of the closet. After Katherine placed Scout and Abra in one carrier, Iris appeared out of the kitchen and ran to that carrier's door. The Siamese was shaking and had her tail between her legs.

"It's okay, Miss Siam," Katherine said, putting her inside. Iris began washing Abra's face.

Daryl came in. "How can I help?"

Katherine said with a trembling voice, "I have two more cats to find. I think I know where they are." She handed Daryl the second cat carrier and walked back to the living room. She avoided the location where Jake and Patricia had been shot and moved to the front of the room, where Abby's and Iris's favorite wingback chair was located. She got down on her knees and gently felt inside the torn chair lining under the seat until she felt a cat. She brought it out. It was a terrified Abby. She kissed her on the head, then placed her inside the carrier. Reaching back again into the chair, she found Lilac, who was quivering.

"Me-yowl," she cried.

"It's okay, Lilac. Calm down, sweetie." She cradled the upset Siamese next to her chest, kissed her, then placed her next to the Abyssinian.

Once the cats were safe in their carriers, Daryl said emphatically, "Katz, we've got to get them out of here. This is a crime scene."

"Can you take Mum, Colleen and my cats to the bungalow I own? It's two houses down from Cokey's and Margie's."

"Yes, I know where it is," he said, then to Colleen, "Pack a bag. I'll come back for you and your mom."

Katherine walked back to the kitchen and removed the bungalow keys, which were hanging on a key hook mounted on the wall. She went back and handed them to Daryl. "The cat's room is the second bedroom on the right. When you get there, let them out, but first make sure the bedroom door is closed. I don't want them running amok in the house."

"Will do. Katz, listen, as soon as I can, I'll bring Colleen to the hospital. Jake's in good hands. The trauma center is the best in the state."

Tears started streaming down Katherine's face. "Thank you," she choked.

Chapter Nine

Jake's mom and dad — Johnny and Cora —
drove up to the mansion in their extended cab
pickup. Katherine was waiting for them on the front
step — shivering. She'd forgotten her coat. It
seemed like an eternity before they got there. Daryl
had already taken the cats to the bungalow and had
just returned to take Mrs. Murphy and Colleen there,
as well. He shouted from his car, "Everything's
okay." Katherine shouted back, "Thanks!" She was
impatient to get to the hospital. Johnny got out and
opened the passenger door. Katherine stepped up,
slid over and sat down. She said hello to Jake's
mom, but Cora didn't answer. She sat up front with a
box of Kleenex on her lap. Johnny got back in and
pulled out onto Lincoln Street.

"I'm so sorry it took us so long, but we were
half-way to the city when we got the call," Johnny
apologized. "Jake was just at our house."

Cora began crying. "We were planning our Christmas dinner . . . " her voice trailed off into silence.

Johnny finished, "Every Christmas, the Cokenbergers get together for dinner and afterward exchange gifts. Jake asked if it was okay if he brought you, and we said of course. It would be our pleasure."

Katherine said, "How sweet! I'd love to go."

Cora said sadly, "In the past, Jake always brought Victoria, but when she passed away, he just went to pieces. He adored her." Victoria was Jake's wife, who died from cancer. Katherine suspected Cora and Victoria had been very close.

"My son thinks the world of you," Johnny countered. "He talks about you all the time."

Katherine didn't answer. She didn't want to engage in any conversation. She just wanted to quietly look out at the snowy landscape. Her head was still throbbing from the loud gunshots. Her mind was racing with dozens of tumbling, disorganized thoughts, but one thought was like a steady drumbeat beneath the mental noise. *I've just killed someone*, she thought.

Johnny read her mind. He didn't talk again until they got to the city. A long line of cars were stalled outside of town. "Damn, Christmas shoppers," he complained.

Cora scolded, "Watch your mouth."

The cars began to slowly pull forward.

Cora started crying again. No matter what her husband said to try to console her, it clearly wasn't working. Once they arrived at the hospital, Johnny let the two women off at the Emergency entrance, then pulled into the parking lot to find a spot. Reuniting in the hospital lobby, the group headed for the front desk, where a busy receptionist directed them to another part of the building. They found the waiting room and walked in. Curiously, Mark Dunn was sitting on one of the chairs against the windowed wall.

When he saw Katherine, he stood up.

"Mark," she said, surprised. "How did you know?"

"Chief London called. I was filing some papers down at the courthouse when I got the call. I thought you'd like some company."

"Thank you. That was sweet."

"Good to see you, Mark," Johnny said, shaking Mark's hand.

Cora looked at Mark and Katherine suspiciously, as if they had a thing for each other.

Mark led Katherine to a different part of the waiting room. "Let's sit here," he suggested.

People started coming in and swarming around Johnny and Cora. Katherine assumed they were members of Jake's huge, extended family.

Mark began, "Hasn't been the best month for either one of us."

Katherine nodded back at him without speaking.

"I'm so sorry about Jake. He's a good man," he said, then whispered, "I regret looking so hard to find you. I'm beginning to think the Colfax fortune is a big curse — "

"Shhh," Katherine interrupted. "If you hadn't have found me, I would have never met Jake. I'm in love with him, Mark."

"I think the feeling is mutual," Mark said, taking her hand. "I'm very happy for you."

"The chief probably also told you I shot Patricia."

"Yes, he did. I'm sorry, Katz. You did what you had to do. How did she get in? Is there something wrong with the new security system?"

"The problem is there's a manual override named Mrs. Murphy. Maybe Patricia tried to get inside and it set off the alarm. Mum turned it off and answered the door."

"Wow, wasn't a scholarly moment on Mrs. Murphy's part. I know it's probably not the time and place," Mark said hesitantly, "but I've been meaning to call you about Robbie Brentwood."

"What's up? Maybe it will get my mind off of things for a few minutes."

"You were right to be suspicious of Robbie. I owe you an apology. I'm sorry I didn't trust your instincts."

Katherine didn't answer. She thought he should have said he *never* trusted her instincts.

Mark continued, "I just found out the FBI was closing in to arrest him. It seems there really wasn't a specialized mutual fund in New York. It was just a clever Ponzi scheme."

"I tried to warn you," Katherine said solemnly. "The pic Colleen took in Manhattan — the one I texted you — had 'red' flag written all over it."

"Dozens of Erie residents were bilked out of their hard-earned savings."

"How about you? What did you lose?"

"A lot." Mark looked down at his hands and nervously wrung them.

"I hesitate to ask this question, but did you invest any of my great aunt's estate money in Robbie's scheme? Am I poor now?"

"Well, I wouldn't exactly say you were poor. You still have five million."

"I take that to mean yes, you did," she said.

After a long, awkward pause, Mark said, "I don't have legal access to your great aunt's money, so the answer is no. The bank's trust department always controlled investment of the estate assets and believe me, they are very conservative. I didn't invest any of your soon-to-be inheritance."

Katherine felt relief. She had plans for the fortune and wanted to spend it to help others.

"But there will be a happy ending to this mess. I think Robbie didn't know the New York investors were ripping people off. I think he genuinely believed that the mutual fund was the real deal, at least until very recently."

Katherine rolled her eyes and said, "No way."

"Robbie deposited nearly all the money from the most recent investors into a separate account, payable to his mother upon his death. The bank notified Elizabeth this morning and she contacted me. She is adamant about returning the money. She's authorized the bank and me to take care of this. Hopefully, everyone in Erie who invested will be reimbursed. She's devastated that she lost her son — her only child. And she's convinced of his innocence."

"I'm sorry for her loss," Katherine said. "I won't feel relieved until Cokey gets his kids' college fund back. Mark, I hope you get your money back as well."

A doctor came in and asked for Jake's parents. Johnny and Cora followed the woman to the door, then surprisingly, Cora stopped and called for Katherine.

Katherine bounced up from her seat and hurried over to them.

The doctor introduced herself, "I'm Dr. Ruby McDermond. Let's move into a private room so we can talk." She motioned the three to step into a small, windowless consulting room. She quietly shut the door. Cora looked like she was going to faint, so Katherine moved to her side and took her by the arm.

"Please sit down, Cora," Katherine said. Johnny pulled out a chair and Cora slid into the seat. Johnny stood behind her with his hands placed reassuringly on her shoulders. Katherine leaned against the wall.

Dr. McDermond began, "The trauma surgery team cleaned up the wound and checked for bullet fragments. The bullet did not hit a major artery and made a clean exit through the shoulder muscle. He's out of surgery and being taken to the ICU. He's still in shock, which typically happens in gunshot victims, but he should stabilize soon. I'll let you know when you can see him."

"When will that be?" Cora asked. "I need to see him now!"

Dr. McDermond shook her head. "He's still under the anesthesia. I'll let you know." She left the room.

Cora began sobbing again. "Oh, Johnny, how could this happen? He was just at our house. He was so happy. Then, he goes over to *her* house," she said venomously with an angry side glance at Katherine.

"Cora, stop it. Right now!" Johnny demanded. "Katherine has been through hell. Think of someone else besides yourself for a change."

Not wanting to hear anything else, Katherine raced out of the room and nearly collided with Colleen, who had just arrived with Daryl.

"Katz! What's wrong?" Colleen asked.

Katherine collected herself. "Jake's out of surgery and being taken to a room in the ICU."

Daryl spoke gently. "Katz, I can show you where the ICU waiting room is. It has limited seating, so my big family will have to either hang out here or go home. Give me a second. I need to tell my family this."

Daryl said, "Listen up, folks. The docs have patched Jake up. He's in recovery and being moved to the ICU. I think it's best that everyone go home now." Jake's father, Johnny, added, "Thank you for coming. I'll let you all know more about his condition tomorrow." Most of the Cokenbergers cleared the room along with Mark Dunn, who nodded at Katherine, "Text me!" he mouthed the words. Grandpa Cokenberger refused to go, "I ain't goin' till I hear my grandson is gonna be all right."

Johnny said to the stubborn grandfather, "Okay, Dad, let's go to the ICU waiting room."

Daryl returned to Katz and Colleen and took them both by the arm. He led them to another wing in the hospital.

They walked in silence for a few minutes, then Daryl asked, "Katz, do you know if the bullet was removed?"

Katherine nodded. "The doctors also checked for bullet fragments."

"That's good. Now we have to pray he doesn't get an infection."

"I know," Katherine agreed. She turned to Colleen. "Is Mum all right? She was pretty shaken back there."

Colleen's face clouded, "Mum is fine once she sobers up. She wants to go home tomorrow. Daryl and I are taking her to the airport. Katz, I called Jacky on the way over here. He's taking her somewhere in Manhattan for help. This drinking business has to stop."

"Colleen, I think that's an excellent plan. Are you flying out, too?"

"I'm staying until Jake gets released from the hospital, and I don't want to hear any argument about it."

"Thanks, you're a dear friend."

Katherine asked Daryl, "Did my kids give you any trouble when you got them to the bungalow?"

"They were pretty shook up when I got there, but once I let them out in their room, they seemed to be okay."

"Thank you for taking them over there."

"You're welcome," Daryl said. "Here we are," he said, pointing to the waiting area. "You two have a seat. I'll let the nurse at the desk know we're here." As Daryl walked out, Johnny, Cora and Grandpa Cokenberger came in. Cora sat as far away from Katherine as she could. In a few minutes, Daryl returned with a cardboard tray with six steaming cups of coffee. He said to Katherine, "Colleen and I plan on camping out here with you. When we find out Jake's been stabilized, I'll take the two of you home."

Katherine managed a smile. "Thank you."

*　　*　　*

It was two o'clock in the morning before a nurse came in and said Jake was awake. "Is there a Katherine in the room?" she asked.

Katherine startled, then said, "I'm Katherine."

"Jake is asking for you. Would you like to follow me?"

Cora jumped out of her seat and ran for the door. "He's my son. I demand to see him right this minute!" Johnny rushed over and clutched her arm. "Let's do what Jake wants. Okay?" Cora wrenched her arm back. Her eyes threw a cold dagger at Katherine.

Colleen said under her breath, "Lighten up, lady."

Katherine got up hesitantly from her seat, then followed the nurse.

"Hi, I'm Jake's nurse. My name is Ramona. He's still very groggy, but he's coherent enough to be asking for you."

Katherine felt a quick adrenaline rush and then felt faint. She felt as if her legs were going to give out. Slowly, she walked into Jake's hospital room. She was trembling so much she couldn't speak. The nurse found her a chair and placed it next to Jake's bed. She gently sat down.

"Come closer," he whispered.

Katherine leaned over. A tear slid down her cheek.

"Are you okay?" he asked weakly.

"Yes, but you're the one who got shot." Katherine flinched when she saw the bandages covering his wound.

"Are the cats okay?"

"Yes, they're fine. Daryl took them to the bungalow."

"What about that Marston woman?" His voice became weaker.

"Jake," Katherine said, bringing her hand up to stifle a sob. "I shot her."

"Is she dead?"

"Yes."

"It was self-defense, Katz. I know you feel terrible about this, but there was no other choice. She would have killed you."

Katherine shook her head. "I know."

"I want you to go home now and get some rest. I'm in good hands." He turned his head and fell back to sleep.

The nurse said, "That's to be expected. We'll let him rest now."

"Can I leave my number where you can reach me?"

The nurse wrote down Katherine's number. "And when you call the hospital, ask for the ICU, then ask for me. I'll be here all night until eight in the morning."

Katherine smiled and went back to the waiting room. Daryl and Colleen were standing outside. Daryl said, "I'm sort of the family spokesperson and referee."

Colleen said tartly, "Yes, if I stayed in that room a moment longer with Jake's mother, I would have —"

Katherine interrupted. "It's okay, carrot top. Jake asked me to go home, so that's where I'm heading."

Daryl said, "After you left, Aunt Cora made a scene and went to the front desk. She talked to a doctor who explained that Jake was out of danger. So, I'll take the two of you home now. I'll drop Grandpa off on the way."

"What about Cora and Johnny? Are they staying?" Katherine asked.

Daryl rubbed his brow. "Aunt Cora won't leave until she talks to her son."

"That's understandable. I'm ready when you are," Katherine said.

Daryl went inside the room and returned with Grandpa Cokenberger. The four walked out of the hospital. It was snowing lightly and the wind had kicked up. The parking lot was nearly empty. Everyone had their coats on except Katherine. Grandpa Cokenberger came over and said, "Where's your coat, sweet pea?"

"Jake calls me that," Katherine said sadly.

The burly, elderly man hugged her and said, "Welcome to the family! I insist you wear my coat." He draped the coat over Katherine's shoulders.

She gazed ahead at Daryl and Colleen holding hands. She thought at that moment in time, all was right in the world. She basked in the glow that Jake was going to be okay.

*　　*　　*

Daryl parked his classic Impala in front of the bungalow and the three got out.

"I'm exhausted," Katherine said. She gazed at the front of the house. Mrs. Murphy had turned on the overhead porch light. The living room light was on, too. Scout and Abby stood tall in the window, watching the group climb the steps to the front porch.

Katherine said to Daryl, "Thank you so much for everything."

"My pleasure," Daryl said. He smiled, said good-night, and left. Katherine opened the door. As Colleen and she entered the house, three cats surrounded them.

"Oh, Katz, I don't know why they're out," Colleen said. "Daryl said he locked them in their room."

Mrs. Murphy, wearing a fleece nightgown with rollers in her hair, came in. "Katz, is Jake all right? I haven't been able to sleep a wink."

"Yes, he's out of danger now," Katherine answered coldly. She was annoyed at Mum for a number of things, and now she had one more thing to add to her list.

Mrs. Murphy apologized. "I'm so sorry. I hope you forgive me. The cats were makin' so much noise, I let them out. Then I gave them a bit of food and they quieted down. If I didn't know any better, I think they've been pacin' the floor and lookin' out the windows waitin' for you."

"Thanks for feeding them." Katherine sat down on the floor and said to the cats, "Can I have a group hug? I really need one."

"Waugh," Scout cried. With Abra and Iris she ran over and circled Katherine. Lilac and Abby trotted out of their room and collapsed against their person. Katherine pulled them close and embraced them for a moment.

Observing Katherine's private moment, Colleen led her mother to the kitchen.

Once they cleared the room, Katherine said to the cats, "Jake is going to be okay, but you guys probably already knew that."

"Raw," Abra said sweetly. Iris reached up and bit Katherine lightly on the ear.

"Thank you, Miss Siam. I needed that."

Lilac and Abby wanted to be held. "That might be hard to do." Katherine leaned forward and kissed each one of them on the head.

"Okay, it's time to go to bed. I'll join you shortly." Katherine got up and made her way to her bedroom. The cats followed and jumped on top of the bed. She hurriedly locked them in.

She then went to the kitchen. Mrs. Murphy sat across from Colleen at the built-in table in the breakfast nook. She wore a worried expression on her face. She began in a low voice, "Katz, you know I think the world of you. Never in this life would I want anythin' to happen to you. I've made so many mistakes today."

Katherine turned and switched on the counter light. She was quiet and didn't answer.

"For starters, I should have never let that deranged woman in. If this woman would have come to my door in Queens, I wouldn't have even opened the door. I keep askin' myself, 'What was I thinkin'? Why did I let her in?'"

Colleen muttered under-her-breath, "You were drunk, Mum!"

Katherine finally said, "Patricia is — was — very persuasive. She was an excellent liar. But Mum, why didn't you stay in your room when I told you not to come out until I'd let you know? You could have been killed, popping into the living room like that."

"I heard the shots. I just wanted to help you."

"What about the cats? Why were they out when I got home? Why did you let them out of their room when I specifically asked you to leave them in there? They could have been shot by that nutcase. And you just did it again. Daryl locked them in, but *you* let them out. It's like you don't respect my wishes."

"I do respect your wishes. I'm so sorry. I'm leavin' tomorrow. I know you're angry at me, but I want you to know I love you very much. You've been like a daughter to me," Mrs. Murphy choked and started to cry.

Colleen said, "Mum, please don't cry. We're *all* really tired. Let's just call it a day."

Katherine said, "Yes, let's do. I plan on getting some sleep and then going back to the hospital. Colleen, what time are you leaving to take Mum to the airport?"

"She's got a ten o'clock flight. Daryl is picking us up at seven-thirty."

Katherine walked over to Mum and touched her hand. "I *am* angry, but I also love you, too. In time we can talk about other things." Then she said to Colleen, "Get me up when you leave. I want to say good-bye."

"Okay. Good night, Katz."

"Good night." Katherine walked to her room and found five cats curled in a single, breathing fur pile. She crawled beside them and went to sleep with her nose burrowed in Scout's back.

Chapter Ten

As she climbed the stairs, Katherine juggled a wooden tray with a bowl of soup, a fresh bottle of water, and Jake's medicine. He was recuperating at the pink mansion in her bedroom with the tall, renaissance-revival bed. Cokey built a two-level stair unit to sit flush against the bed so Jake could climb up and out of bed. Jake used a cane to help him with his balance.

The state police informed Katherine they were finished with their evidence gathering and that she could move back into the mansion. The mauve loveseat had been taken into evidence, together with the Belter chair Robbie Brentwood had been so fond of. Katherine said she didn't want them back. They also suggested she hire a professional cleaning company to thoroughly clean the living room. Before Patricia's death in the mansion, Katherine didn't know such services existed. She mistakenly thought the police took care of that. But they didn't.

Katherine wouldn't leave the bungalow and move back into the house until the cleaning crew was finished. She closed the pocket doors to the room and refused to go in there. Cokey installed hook and eye locks, up high, to also prevent the cats from entering. She'd asked Margie to come up with a design plan to incorporate the Victorian features with new furnishings. But she couldn't get rid of the wingback chair. Katherine knew there were two cat rules to strictly obey. Never give up Iris's and Abby's favorite wingback chair, and never throw out Lilac's bear, no matter how tattered the stuffed toy had become.

Abby followed her into the bedroom, chirping sweetly. Ever since Patricia Marston had tried to kill her a second time, she clung to Katherine. Lilac was following close behind.

Katherine found Jake sitting up in bed. "Look at you! How long have you been up?" she asked.

He closed the cover to his laptop. "Come here," he said, patting the bed.

Katherine placed the tray on the dresser, then climbed up onto the tall bed and joined him, carefully sitting next to him. Their backs leaned against the headboard. Lilac and Abby jumped on the bed and launched onto the high pediment of the headboard. They peered down at the couple with interest.

"It was hard to sit up, but I did it," he said.

"What are you doing online? Surfing the web?" she asked with a sparkle in her eye.

"I was reading my email. I'm officially on leave of absence until the doctor approves my going back to work. The Dean already has an adjunct professor lined up to teach my classes in two weeks, when the students come back from break."

"I brought you some homemade potato soup. Courtesy of Colleen, who insisted on using fresh potatoes."

Jake teased, "Oh, she flew to Ireland to dig them up."

Katherine moved to get the soup, but Jake caught her arm. "Would it hurt Colleen's feelings if I didn't eat it just now. I'm not really hungry. You can warm it up for me later, if you don't mind."

"Okay. You're due for another pain pill in about an hour."

Jake said, "It's strange how the pain knows when to rear its ugly head right before its time to take the next pill. Oh, well." He sighed. "I want to show you something funny." Jake reopened his laptop. He keyed in the URL for the *Erie Herald* web page. Then he scrolled to December 13 — the date of the holiday fundraiser. The reporter/photographer Russell Krow had taken a series of pictures of Lilac flying from the cat carrier to the cake table.

Katherine started laughing. "You probably know what this publicity means?"

"What's that, sweet pea?"

"Lilac and I will be banned from the next event."

They looked at a few more pictures, then Jake shut down the computer and pushed it aside. "While you were at the drugstore getting my meds — thank you very much, Nurse Katz — I had several brown-masked visitors."

"Really," she said, amused. She reached over and took his hand, intertwining her fingers with his. "Let me guess: Iris, Scout, and Abra?"

"Just Scout and Abra."

"And what did you and your visitors have to talk about?"

"The girls said I should go for it!"

"Go for what?" Katherine smiled. "What have you guys been up to?"

"Okay," Jake began slowly. "Katz, I know they're *special*."

"Of course they're special. They used to be stage performers," she joked.

"I know that," he said with a wry smile. "I think your cats, not just Scout and Abra, have . . . special abilities."

Katherine grew very serious. Her eyes grew very big and she turned to face him. "How are they special?" She wondered if Jake knew about their extraordinary gifts.

"The day I got shot and I was lying wounded on the floor, I was aware of you and the cats surrounding me with — I don't know how to explain it — a great sense of love. Maybe it was the shock or loss of blood, but I felt connected to *all* of you. I couldn't speak. I couldn't open my eyes, but I *sensed* you."

Katherine squeezed his hand. "We were there. We surrounded you."

There was a long silence.

Jake broke it. "I want to ask you something very important to me, but it requires helpers."

"Feline helpers? Let me guess. When you get better you're going to bake me another cake?"

Jake smiled his famous Cokenberger grin. "Scout! Abra!" he said in the loudest voice he could muster, considering his healing shoulder wound.

Katherine heard the jiggling of a bell in the hallway. When she turned to follow the sound, Abra came through the door and jumped up onto the bed. She wore a rhinestone collar with a bell on it. There was a small velvet-covered box clamped in her jaws. She dropped it in Katherine's lap. "Raw," she said, closing her eyes and blinking a kiss. Scout hopped up next to her and nudged Katherine's hand.

Jake said, "Well, open it!"

Katherine slowly opened the box. Inside a diamond ring gleamed in the light of the ceiling chandelier. A happy tear slid from her eye.

Jake said, "I love you. I will always love you. And I want to spend the rest of my life with you. Katz, will you marry me?"

Before Katherine could answer, the rowdy cries of five cats were ear-piercing. Lilac and Abby took long leaps from the top of the headboard to the foot of the bed, and began prancing figure eights on the bedspread, me-yowling and chirping happily. Iris joined them and belted out a couple of yowls. Scout stood up on her hind feet and put her paws on Katherine's shoulders. She cried "waugh" right in Katherine's ear.

"Yes," Katherine answered through the noisy din. "But, Jake, you must understand."

"What's that?" he asked, smiling.

"I come with cats!"

"Chirp," Abby cried as if to say, "Kiss her, you fool."

With difficulty Jake leaned over and kissed Katherine tenderly on the lips. The cats became very quiet.

"I love you, too," she said. "Jake, you're the best thing that ever happened to me."

"Me, too," he said, winking. "Now curl up here. I'm suddenly very sleepy. I need to take a nap."

Before she had time to climb out of bed to switch off the ceiling fixture, Scout leaped onto the bedside table, reached up with her long, slender brown paw, and turned the light off.

"Ma-waugh," she cried, and the other cats followed her out of the room.

THE END

Dear Reader . . .

Thank you so much for reading my book. I hope you enjoyed reading it as much as I did writing it. If you liked *"The Cats that Played the Market,"* I would be so thankful if you'd help others enjoy this book, too, by recommending it to your friends, family and book clubs, and/or by writing a positive review on Amazon and/or Goodreads.

I love it when my readers write to me. If you'd like to email me about what you'd like to see in the next book, or just talk about your favorite scenes and characters, email me at: karenannegolden@gmail.com

Amazon author page: http://tinyurl.com/mkmpg4d

My Facebook author page is: https://www.facebook.com/karenannegolden

Website: http://www.karenannegolden.webs.com

Thanks again!

Karen Anne Golden

The Cats that Surfed the Web

Book One in *The Cats that . . .* Cozy Mystery series

If you haven't read the first book, *The Cats that Surfed the Web*, you can download the Kindle version on Amazon at: http://amzn.com/B00H2862YG

Forty four million dollars. A Victorian mansion. And a young career woman with cats. The prospect sounded like a dream come true; what could possibly go wrong?

How could a friendly town's welcome turn into a case of poisoning, murder, and deceit? When Katherine "Katz" Kendall, a computer professional in New York City, discovers she's the sole heir of a huge inheritance, she can't believe her good fortune. She's okay with the clauses of the will: Move to the small town of Erie, Indiana, check. Live in her great aunt's pink Victorian mansion and take care of an Abyssinian cat, double-check.

With her three Siamese cats and best friend, Colleen, riding shotgun, Katz leaves Manhattan to find a former housekeeper dead in the basement. Ghostly intrusions convince Colleen, a card-carrying "ghost hunter," that the mansion is haunted. Several townspeople are furious because Katherine's benefactor promised them the fortune, then changed her will at the last minute. But who would be greedy enough to get rid of the rightful heir to take the money and run? Four adventurous felines help Katz solve the crimes by serendipitously "searching" the Internet for clues.

The Cats that Chased the Storm

Book Two in *The Cats that . . .* Cozy Mystery series

The second book, *The Cats that Chased the Storm*, is also available on Kindle and in paperback. Amazon: http://amzn.com/B00IPOPJOU

It's early May in Erie, Indiana, and the weather has turned most foul. We find Katherine "Katz" Kendall, heiress to the Colfax fortune, living in a pink mansion, caring for her three Siamese and Abby the Abyssinian. Severe thunderstorms frighten the cats, but Scout is better than any weather app. A different storm is brewing, however, with a discovery that connects great-uncle William Colfax to the notorious gangster John Dillinger. Why is the Erie Historical Society so eager to get William's personal papers? Is the new man in Katherine's life a fortune hunter? Will Abra mysteriously reappear, and is Abby a magnet for danger?

A fast-paced whodunit, the second book in "The Cats that" series involves four extraordinary felines that help Katz unravel the mysteries in her life.

The Cats that Told a Fortune

Book Three in *The Cats that . . .* Cozy Mystery series

If you haven't read the third book, *The Cats that Told a Fortune*, you can download the Kindle version on Amazon at:
http://amzn.com/B00MAAZ3ZU

Autumn in Erie, Indiana means crisp, cool days of adventure. Katherine "Katz" Kendall — heiress to a fortune — settles into her late great aunt's Victorian mansion with her high-spirited feline companions. What better time to host a Halloween party?

Katz sets the stage with spooky decorations, a fortune teller, and even a magician. Scout — a Siamese with extraordinary abilities — fang marks a "Wheel of Fortune" Tarot card. Is it because her person will soon receive millions, or does that card have a more ominous meaning? Although Iris is smitten with the Russian charmer, it's unclear whether he's a lovable rogue, or an opportunistic thief. Katz's new boyfriend Jake and best friend Colleen join in the fun.

Along the way, Katz and her cats uncover important clues to the identity of a serial killer, and Katz finds out about Erie's crime family . . . the hard way.

This fun, fast-paced third book in "The Cats that . . . Cozy Mystery" series involves five extraordinary felines that help Katz solve a crime.